Our acclaimed and esteemed friend's most gracious gift arrived four days ago. What a wonderful treasure! And yet, alas, its very possession brings with it an equal measure of danger.

"Lay not up for yourselves treasures upon earth, where moth and rust doth corrupt, and where thieves break through and steal: But lay up for yourselves treasures in heaven, where neither moth nor rust doth corrupt, and where thieves do not break through nor steal."

Prudence Willard's Journal
Matthew 6:19–20
August 21, 1886

SECRETS OF WAYFARERS INN

Family Secrets
River of Life
All That Remains
Greater than Gold
A Flame in the Night
Never the Twain Shall Meet

SECRETS OF WAYFARERS INN

Never the Twain Shall Meet

BETH ADAMS WITH
E. E. KENNEDY

Guideposts
New York

Secrets of Wayfarers Inn is a trademark of Guideposts.

Published by Guideposts Books & Inspirational Media
110 William Street
New York, NY 10038
Guideposts.org

Copyright © 2018 by Guideposts. All rights reserved.

This book, or parts thereof, may not be reproduced, stored in a retrieval system, or transmitted in any form or by any means, electronic, mechanical, photocopying, recording, or otherwise, without the written permission of the publisher.

This is a work of fiction. Marietta, Ohio, actually exists, and some characters may be based on actual residents whose identities have been fictionalized to protect their privacy. Apart from the actual people, events, and locales that figure into the fiction narrative, all other names, characters, businesses, and events are the creation of the author's imagination or are used fictitiously.

Every attempt has been made to credit the sources of copyrighted material used in this book. If any such acknowledgment has been inadvertently omitted or miscredited, receipt of such information would be appreciated.

Scripture references are from the following sources: *The Holy Bible*, King James Version (KJV). *The Holy Bible, New International Version*. Copyright ©1973, 1978, 1984, 2011 by Biblica, Inc. Used by permission of Zondervan. All rights reserved worldwide. www.zondervan.com

Cover and interior design by Müllerhaus
Cover illustration by Bob Kayganich, represented by Deborah Wolfe, LTD.
Typeset by Aptara, Inc.

Printed and bound in the United States of America
10 9 8 7 6 5 4 3 2 1

For where your treasure is, there will your heart be also.
Matthew 6:21 KJV

Chapter One

Tess Wallace sipped a cup of strong dark coffee and held her breath as Jack Willard jumped down the last three stairs. The three-year-old was adorable, with his dark hair and big blue eyes, but he had more energy than he knew what to do with. The boy landed with a thud, hooted his excitement, and then ran into the café, where Winnie was just writing out the menu on the large chalkboard. Well, hopefully none of their other guests had been trying to sleep in this morning. Sharon, the boy's mother, was halfway down the stairs, tiny Sadie tucked into a sling against her chest.

"I'm so sorry," Sharon said, nodding toward the boy, who was scrambling onto a chair in the café. There were dark half-moons under her eyes. The baby must have kept her up last night. Tess's own children were grown and her daughter, Lizzie, had children of her own, but Tess still shuddered when she thought about the overwhelming exhaustion of those first few months. "I told him to go down quietly, but..."

"He's three," Tess said. "I have three grandchildren his age, so I totally understand."

"Three of them?" Sharon's eyes widened. Tess could just make out the infant's downy head poking out the top of the sling.

"Triplets." Tess nodded. "Two boys and a girl."

"Oh wow." Sharon laughed and shook her head. "Oh wow."

"They're a huge blessing, but they're quite a handful." Tess thought for a moment about their sweet faces, with their big brown eyes and sandy-colored hair. Sweet Liam, Henry, and Harper. She missed those little imps. "Anyway, I understand about the futility of trying to convince a three-year-old to walk anywhere when he could just as easily run."

"Thank you for understanding. I just hope the other guests aren't too put out."

"You're kind to worry. But for now, just enjoy your breakfast. You look like you could use it."

"Thank you. I'd read that the hospitality in this place was out of this world, but you've really gone above and beyond. Those granola bars you provide in the room saved me in the middle of the night."

"I'm so glad." Tess watched as the tired young mother headed into the café, ordered her young son to stop standing on the chair, and sat down across from him.

Tess and her friends Janice and LuAnn had opened this inn with the intention of ministering to their guests, and she was happy to hear that Sharon was enjoying her stay. But Tess was still a little unclear on why, exactly, this family had chosen Wayfarers Inn for their visit. Everyone was welcome here, of course, and they appreciated all the guests who graced their doors, especially as they were still getting the place up and running. But she would have thought a family with young children might be more comfortable at one of the chain hotels in the area that offered suites and indoor pools and arcades. And, she thought as Jack banged his knife against the glass-topped table, their other guests no doubt might be as well.

The café wasn't even officially open yet, but the sweet smell of cinnamon and sugar wafted out of the kitchen. Taylor appeared at Sharon's side and deposited a cup of coffee and a coloring book with crayons, unrequested, and Tess thanked God they'd found him. For a busy college student, the young man had a strong sense of what their guests needed and how best to serve them.

Tess turned back to the iPad in front of her and reviewed the list of upcoming bookings. The reservations slowed down over the next two weeks, but then they picked up again the week of Thanksgiving. There were already six rooms booked for that weekend, and the amount of traffic to the section of their website that showed available rooms indicated that there might be more bookings coming in soon. Praise God. Tess knew that the first year of an inn's life was critical, and so far it looked like they just might make it.

"Excuse me?"

Tess looked up to find Sharon's husband, Moses, standing in front of the check-in desk. He was tall, with thick dark hair. Probably in his midthirties, if she had to guess. His blue eyes were striking against his bronzed skin.

"I'm so sorry. I didn't see you come down."

"That's quite all right. I'm sorry to bother you."

"You're not bothering me. This is my job." She set the iPad down and flashed him a smile. "What can I help you with?"

"I have something of a strange question."

"My favorite kind."

He looked around, and then he pulled something from his pocket. A small piece of paper, folded over.

"This was slipped under the door of our room late last night. I was wondering if you or your business partners saw anyone in the hallways. Or if you have security cameras or anything like that." He was looking around the lobby, scanning for... well, she had no idea for what.

"Goodness." Tess shook her head. "I'm afraid we don't have security cameras here. And I was up in my room by eight, so I didn't see anything. I can ask my partners, though."

"Thank you. That would be great." He put the paper back in his pocket.

"Is everything okay?" Whatever was on that paper was troubling him, that much was clear.

"Yes. It's..." He looked around again and then back at Tess. It was almost as if he were trying to read her, the way he studied her face. Then he seemed to come to some sort of decision.

"It's kind of strange, really." He took the paper back out, unfolded it, and held it out so she could see it. It was a note, handwritten, on one of the pads with the Wayfarers Inn logo that they placed in each guest room.

I have the SLC treasure, the note read. *Leave a cashier's check for $50,000 in an envelope behind the painting in the lobby and wait for further instructions.*

"Wow." Tess read the note again, just to make sure she'd seen it correctly. "What in the world does it mean?"

Moses sighed and shifted his weight from one foot to the other. He looked around again, and then he gave a little half-shrug.

"I got a strange note in the mail a few weeks ago too," he said. He reached into his pocket again, this time pulling out a business-sized envelope. It was addressed to Moses Willard in Cleveland, and the return address space was blank. He opened the envelope and pulled out a single piece of white paper printed from a computer.

Moses—
Do the letters SLC mean anything to you?
The treasure that was stolen from your family has been recovered. If you want to know more about it, come to the Wayfarers Inn in Marietta, Ohio, on November 5 and wait for further instructions.

"What in the world?" Tess pulled the note closer to her and read it again, but it still didn't make any sense. "What does it mean? What treasure is he talking about? What is SLC?"

She looked up and realized he was studying her again.

"I can promise you, I don't know a thing about this." She pushed the letter back toward him. He couldn't really think... "And neither do my business partners, I assure you."

"No." He leaned back and shook his head. "Judging by your reaction, I don't think you do. I don't think anyone could fake that confusion."

She wasn't sure whether to be relieved or offended, but she was too curious to dwell on it. "Do you have any idea what this is all about?"

Moses didn't say anything for a moment, and then he sighed. "I'll tell you what. Would you mind if I talked about it with all three of you? I need some coffee. I can grab some if you wouldn't mind calling your business partners together. Then I can explain it to all of you at once."

"That sounds like a great idea."

Tess walked over to the service elevator and pressed the button and a moment later, she was stepping out onto the fourth floor, where their private rooms were located. She knocked on LuAnn's door first. LuAnn was often up early because she helped in the kitchen, but today there was no sound from inside her apartment. Tess knocked harder, and a moment later, a sleepy-eyed LuAnn pulled open the door, knotting a robe around her waist.

"I'm so sorry. I've woken you," Tess said. She could see the morning light slanting in through LuAnn's windows and realized that it was still quite early.

"That's all right. What's going on?"

"One of our guests had a strange note shoved under his door," Tess said. "I think we all need to take a look at it."

LuAnn didn't hesitate. "I'll be right down." She closed the door, and Tess walked over to Janice's room. Janice's door was open and her sitting room empty, but Tess found her in an overstuffed armchair in the corner of the common area, sipping a cup of coffee while she read her Bible.

"Hi there." Janice's blonde curls were pulled back into a ponytail, and she was already dressed for the day in slacks and a light sweater and cozy wool socks.

"I'm sorry to bother you, but I was hoping you could come downstairs for a moment. One of our guests has, well, something of a mystery. Would you come down and hear about it?"

"You had me at mystery." Janice set her coffee on the small walnut side table and closed her Bible, then pushed herself up. "What's going on? Who is it?"

"I'll let him tell us about it."

A few minutes later, they were all seated around a table in the café, looking down at the note that had come in the mail. Moses cradled a mug of coffee in his hands.

"What is the treasure this letter is talking about?" Janice asked.

"And what is SLC?" LuAnn said. "Salt Lake City?"

Tess smiled, seeing that they had the exact same questions she'd had.

"And why did whoever sent this want you to come to this particular inn?" Tess asked. Though, if her hunch was right, she might already have an inkling about that one.

Moses glanced around again—to make sure no one was listening?—before he spoke. The only other people in the vicinity were his wife and Jack, who were eating bowls of steaming hot oatmeal, and sweet Sadie. Tess was pretty sure the tiny baby wouldn't repeat a word. The oatmeal smelled like cinnamon and brown sugar, and it seemed like the perfect way to start this cool fall day.

"There is a legend in my family," Moses said, "about a treasure that was passed down through the generations. But it was stolen almost a hundred years ago, and no one has seen it since. My grandparents talked about it sometimes, saying how much the family had lost when it was stolen. But, I don't know, I always thought it was nothing more than a legend. Then this showed up, and..." He let his voice trail off as he shrugged.

"Are you part of the Willard family that lived in Marietta and helped on the Underground Railroad?" LuAnn said, asking what they all wanted to know. When Tess had seen the name Moses Willard pop up in the reservation system, she'd mentioned it to LuAnn and Janice, and they'd all wondered the same thing. They knew the name Moses Willard. Prudence and Jason Willard—a Quaker couple who'd helped shuttle escaped slaves to freedom through the tunnel beneath the building that was now the inn—had named their baby boy Moses.

"That's right." Moses nodded. "Prudence and Jason Willard were my great-great-great-grandparents. I'm Moses Willard the Fifth, named after their son."

"Wow." Tess couldn't believe it. They were talking to a real live descendant of Prudence Willard. After reading Prudence's diary and learning all they could about the selfless acts in which she had risked her life—and the lives of her family members—to carry out, Tess felt like she knew her. And to see one of her descendants in the flesh—one who carried the name she'd given her own son, no less—made her unexpectedly emotional.

"In that case, you are an especially honored guest," Janice said. "Thank you so much for coming."

"This place is beautiful, and it's wonderful to see how you've honored the history here." Moses took a sip of his coffee. "But—excuse me if this sounds flippant—after getting a note like this, I didn't see how I could stay away."

Tess saw his point. "Tell us more about this treasure."

"That's the thing. I don't really know what it was. My parents didn't know. The story I heard was that it was a gift given to my great-great-great-grandparents and it was of considerable value. They held on to it and passed it down, but it was stolen from a safe in my great-grandparents' store in 1928, and it's never been seen again."

"Something of considerable value?" Tess puzzled over that. There was something pulling at the edge of her mind. Something she'd read.

"It could be anything," Janice said. "You don't know anything more?"

"The only other thing I know was who supposedly gave the gift to Prudence and Jason. And that's why it's always been more than a little hard to believe."

"Who was it?" Tess asked.

Moses paused for a moment before saying, "Mark Twain."

Tess's first instinct was to laugh. Sure. Mark Twain—one of the most famous American writers of all time—had given Prudence and Jason Willard—soft-spoken Quakers who lived on a farm in rural Ohio—a treasure of great worth? And the Queen of England had given them a jeweled tiara as well.

But then LuAnn whispered, "SLC. Samuel Langhorne Clemens."

Surely not. It was preposterous to even contemplate such a thing. And yet, there was still something pulling at the edge of Tess's mind, just out of reach. What was it?

"So you're saying that someone sent you this letter"—LuAnn touched the paper that had been mailed to Moses—"to get you to our inn because of a treasure Mark Twain supposedly gave to your great-great-grandparents."

"You forgot a *great* in there," Janice said with a smile.

"Great-great-great grandparents," LuAnn said.

"That's correct," Moses said. He looked a bit sheepish. He glanced at his wife and kids. Sharon was now holding her phone, taking a picture of Jack eating his oatmeal. "I know. It sounds completely nuts. I get an anonymous note in the mail and pack up and bring my whole family here, on the off chance a family legend is not only true, but that someone who says they have it will show up and give me information about it. I understand how crazy it all sounds."

"But..." Tess could see there was more he wanted to say.

"But, I mean, wouldn't you come?" He shrugged. "If you were in my situation, wouldn't you want to know?"

They all thought about it for a moment, and then they all started nodding.

"I would, especially if that family legend involved Mark Twain." LuAnn, a former English teacher, leaned forward a bit. "He's one of the most fascinating characters in all of American letters."

"And I wouldn't be able to resist the mystery," Janice said. "Even though it's most likely, as you say, nothing more than legend, the idea of solving an old mystery would make me come."

Tess was listening, but on another level, she was elsewhere, paging through faded cursive handwriting in her mind. She'd read something... And then it clicked.

"But it might not just be legend," she said. She got up and went over to the desk drawer where she kept her set of photocopies of Prudence's diary. As she rejoined the group, Tess flipped to the journal's later pages, looking for the passage she was thinking of. She could have sworn it was toward the back. Aha. There it was.

"Look at this." She set the binder on the table and turned it so Moses could read it. "Look at this journal entry."

"Is this..." Moses squinted. "Whose journal is this?"

"This is a copy of Prudence's journal," Janice said. "We found the original here when we bought the inn."

"The original is at the Marietta Underground Railroad Museum, just a few blocks away," Tess added.

"Wow." He looked down at the image and shook his head. "I'd heard she kept a journal, but I assumed that was just another family legend."

"That legend, at least, is very real," Tess said.

"Which makes you wonder about the other one," LuAnn said, raising her eyebrows.

"But look here. Look what it says." Tess pointed to the passage she'd found.

Moses appeared to struggle to make out Prudence's florid handwritten script, but he carefully read: "'Our acclaimed and esteemed friend's most gracious gift arrived four days ago. What a wonderful treasure! And yet, alas, its very possession brings with it an equal measure of danger.'"

"I'd forgotten about that entry," Janice said, shaking her head.

"Do you think she could really be referring to Mark Twain here?" LuAnn asked. "Were Prudence and Jason friends with Mark Twain?"

Moses shrugged. "It seems completely implausible, and my parents didn't put much stock in it, but that's the story."

"But how did they meet him? When did they become friends?" Tess couldn't even begin to wrap her head around this. "What is this gift he gave them?"

"Well, that's why I showed up here," Moses said. "To see if someone out there really does have answers to those questions." He took another sip of his coffee. "I figured, the worst that could happen is we've spent a few days in a great old inn and I get to introduce my wife and children to the city where my family came from. And if someone out there really does know something about the Twain treasure and what happened to it, then I would be crazy not to come."

Tess agreed with him. She would have done exactly the same thing.

"So where's the note that was slipped under your door last night?" LuAnn asked.

He pulled out last night's note and set it on the table, beside the letter that had come in the mail.

Tess reread the note.

I have the SLC treasure. Leave a cashier's check for $50,000 in an envelope behind the painting in the lobby and wait for further instructions.

Tess looked over to the lobby at the painting that sat on the carved mahogany mantel above the fireplace. They'd picked it up at a flea market over the summer, and it showed a steamboat cruising along the river. People on the banks of the river were dressed in Victorian clothes, and the inn—then the Riverfront House—was one of the buildings that was shown in the background. Janice had set an arrangement of dried gourds and fall leaves on the mantel next to it.

"It's a bit presumptuous, isn't it?" LuAnn asked. "To assume you simply have fifty thousand dollars at your disposal?"

Moses shrugged. "I don't have that much cash lying around, that's for sure."

He left it at that, though, which made Tess wonder. It was a princely sum, perfectly and thoroughly out of reach for any of the three of them, who were still stretched to the limit after purchasing the inn. But her husband Jeffrey had managed an exclusive resort on a private golf course, and over the years Tess had had the opportunity to interact with plenty of women who would drop that amount and more in a single trip to Nordstrom. She'd seen men buy a set of golf clubs that cost nearly that much without flinching. Could Moses possibly pay the fee? *Would* he?

"So what are you going to do?" Janice asked.

"I'm not sure." At the table behind him, Jack was now smearing oatmeal on the table with one hand while grabbing for his mother's phone with the other, and Sharon was doing her best to comfort a whimpering Sadie. Moses pushed himself up, walked over to the table, and held out his hands. Sharon gratefully held out the baby, and he took her and cradled her in his arms and sat back down. Tess observed his attentiveness to his wife and children with appreciation. "That's why I was hoping one of you either saw something or that you had security cameras."

"I'm afraid not," LuAnn said. "Do you have any idea what time this note was left under your door?"

"We went to bed by nine, but we were up several times in the night with Sadie." He held her up against his shoulder, and the whimpering stopped. "Sharon got up with her around one, and she said there was nothing there then, but I found it when I got up just after four."

The dead of night, then. The inn doors were locked at eleven, and the only people who would have been around were the three of them and their guests.

"It has to be from someone staying at the inn, then," Tess said.

"Does anyone else have a key?"

"Winnie has the code to the back door," LuAnn said. "But we had the locks changed when we moved in, and I don't believe anyone else has a key."

"And Winnie wouldn't have had anything to do with this." Janice's voice was confident, and Tess agreed with her. But still, they would probably need to ask her, just to be sure.

"And it wasn't any of the three of us," Tess said. She felt confident of that. None of them would have kept a secret like this, and none of them was a good enough actress to be able to pull off the shocked and confused reactions they'd just displayed. Beyond that, though, none of them would do anything to put the inn and its reputation—not to mention the memory of their beloved Prudence—in jeopardy.

"We have guests in four rooms besides yours," Tess said. "So I guess it has to be one of them."

"It's strange to be suspecting one of our guests of something like this," LuAnn said. Tess agreed, but she didn't see what alternative they had.

Janice was examining the note that had been shoved under the door. "This is clearly written on the notepad from the room. I wonder..."

"I wondered the same thing," Tess said.

Moses looked at Janice, and LuAnn tilted her head.

"We should examine the pads in the rooms to see if there's an indentation left by the pen," Janice said.

"Ah. Good thinking," LuAnn said. "When the guests go out, we can do that."

"And look at this," Tess said, pointing to the postmark on the envelope that had been mailed to Moses. "It was mailed from Columbus. So whoever sent it lives there."

"Or was passing through there on October 25," Janice said, pointing out the date stamped on the letter.

"Or drove there specifically to throw off anyone hoping to figure out where the sender lives," LuAnn added.

Tess nodded, deflated. So maybe it wasn't as great a clue as she had hoped.

"We'll figure this thing out," she said, hoping she sounded more confident than she felt. "We just need to pay attention to our guests and see what we can learn."

"We'll ask discreet questions," LuAnn said, nodding. "To find out what they know. One of them has to know something."

"We can do that," Janice said. "But..." She turned to Moses. "Don't you want to involve the police in this? We could call Chief Mayfield. This is extortion."

"I've thought about that," Moses said. He glanced over at his family again. Sharon had given up the fight over the cell phone and was focused on shoveling in her breakfast as quickly as she could, while Jack took pictures of the room and himself with her phone. "But I don't think I want to alert the police. Not yet, anyway. The last thing I want to do is scare off whoever sent this and lose the treasure." He patted Sadie's back gently. "If it even exists, that is."

"I think that's smart," LuAnn said. "And I also think it makes sense to hold off on handing over the money for now, at least until we've had a chance to do some sleuthing."

"Oh, believe me, I am not in any rush to write a check for that much money," Moses said with a laugh. "Especially without knowing if the treasure is real."

"Well, if it is, we'll do everything we can to help you find it," Tess said.

She didn't know if Moses looked more relieved or frightened by that prospect.

Chapter Two

Marietta, Ohio
July 23, 1863

Prudence had received a note that morning. A package was expected tonight. She tried not to fret, tried not to worry, even as the hours ticked by and there was no sign of the arrival. She sat at the little table in the basement, not far from stairs that led to the main floor of Riverfront House. Had she missed the signal?

She'd burned the note as soon as she'd memorized its contents, but now she wished she had it to refer back to. Maybe she'd misread it. Maybe she'd misunderstood. Maybe she was supposed to go to the meeting spot at the river as she usually did and bring the package back herself. But she was sure the note had said she was to wait here and the package would arrive soon after nightfall.

Lord, I pray Thee will protect those who risk their lives this night. Even in the privacy of her own mind, she couldn't be more specific about what was going on. The Lord understood what she was saying.

The night air was stifling, the humidity unbearable. Even down here in the basement, where it was generally cooler than up above, she was sweating, and all she was doing was sitting here. She pulled a handkerchief from her pocket and wiped her forehead. There was no clock down here, but she knew it was getting late. The footsteps on the floor above had stilled, the inn growing quiet as the night advanced.

The candle had burned low, and shadows danced in the corners of the room. She should have brought her book of Scriptures. She needed something to keep her mind off whatever was happening out there. *Lord, keep Jason and Moses safe,* she prayed. *Please give them a restful, untroubled night.*

She knew Jason worried when she did this work. She knew he would have changed places with her if he could have. But she was glad that he was home with young Moses, that they were both out of harm's way—for now, anyway. If things went awry tonight, or any night for that matter, all could be lost.

She heard more footsteps upstairs. The creak of the door as it pushed open. Probably Mr. Siloam, coming to see what was taking so long. No one else knew she was down here—or what was expected.

But as the footsteps started to clunk down the stairs, she heard a noise just past the wooden door at the far end of the room. Someone was inside the tunnel.

Prudence rushed over and stood by the door. She knew better than to open it unless she heard the signal. She waited, holding her breath. There was some kind of scraping inside the tunnel. Was it—? But it had to be the package she'd been told to expect. There was no other alternative.

Mr. Siloam was nearing the bottom of the stairs now, taking them slowly. His gout had made walking difficult of late.

The noises inside the tunnel got closer. She heard breathing, a low cough. Someone was just on the other side of the door now. And then, slowly, five knocks in succession. She gave three knocks back. Then two more sounded from the other side.

That was it, then. This was her cue. Holding her candle aloft, she took up the key ring at her waist and found the right key. As frightened as she always was at these moments, she couldn't imagine how much more fear waited on the other side of the door. The people who showed up, seeking shelter, had no idea what they were going to find, and Prudence always tried to make them feel safe and welcome. Still, her hand shook as she tried to fit the key into the lock. Finally, she got it in and turned it. *Be my hands and my feet,* she prayed. *Be my voice.*

She placed her hand on the doorknob and gently tugged it open. In the dim candlelight, she saw a man's lined face, his eyes wide with fright. He was crouched against the wall of the tunnel, his clothes tattered.

"Please, come in," Prudence said. "Thee are safe here."

The man straightened up and took a halting step. She reached out her hand to steady him, and he shrank back from her touch. She pulled her hand back.

"I'm sorry. Please, come in."

She stepped back, and he emerged from the cramped tunnel and into the dark basement. He was quite tall, she realized, and wide. Built of solid muscle. How had he managed to fit through that narrow tunnel? There was a gash on his arm that looked deep. They'd need to attend to that.

"My name is Prudence," she said. His skin was a deep, rich mahogany, and despite the trials he'd surely faced on his journey, there was something like hope in his eyes.

He nodded, and she closed the door to the tunnel behind him. After she'd locked it back up, she turned to the man.

"This way. You can rest in this room, and I will bring you some—"

He started to turn, but froze, his gaze caught on something by the stairs. His face changed, a mask of fear descending in an instant.

"It's all right," she said. "That's Mr. Siloam. He owns—"

But when she turned to look, she saw that it was not Mr. Siloam at all. It was—

Oh dear Lord.

She felt her strength leave her, and she braced herself against the wall to hold herself up.

It was a man. A guest. A man who—

Oh Father, help us.

She hadn't caught his name but recognized his bushy brown hair and mustache. She'd heard him speaking earlier. A riverboat captain, he'd said. Not a Northerner, for sure. Kentucky or Missouri, given the twang. Unlikely to be friendly toward—well, any of this.

The man stood there, his eyes wide, his face pale in the dark room.

"I—" What could she possibly say that would explain away what he had just witnessed? "We—" She started again, but before she could get another word out, the Southerner turned and fled back up the stairs.

She turned to the man in front of her, the man who had traveled so far and endured so much. The hope had vanished from his eyes. He knew as well as she did that they might have just been discovered.

How much had the other man seen?

Chapter Three

Tess had just gotten back to the check-in desk when Isaiah Sellers came down the stairs a few minutes later. Isaiah was staying in Maple and Mum on the second floor, and he had checked in the previous evening. Tess hadn't been around when he'd arrived, but she'd taken him a toothbrush when he discovered he'd forgotten his before bed, so she'd met him briefly.

"Good morning," she said with a smile as he stepped into the lobby. "Did you sleep well?"

She watched him carefully. Did he glance at the painting over the fireplace? It was hard to say.

"Good morning." Isaiah wore a pressed button-down shirt and slacks with polished leather shoes. "That smells heavenly."

"Winnie's oatmeal is delicious," Tess said. "Make sure you get some before you head out." She looked toward the café, where Sharon and Jack still sat, Jack happily filling Sharon's phone with photos. Moses had taken baby Sadie upstairs.

"I was just about to." He carried a leather briefcase and had reading glasses tucked into his shirt pocket. He turned toward the café, but before he could walk away, Tess tried to engage him.

"Are you enjoying your stay?"

"Oh yes. This hotel is beautiful." He gestured around the lobby. "So charming, and with such a great sense of history."

"Thank you. We've worked hard to make it feel warm and cozy."

"Yes. It's such a nice break from the soulless chain hotels."

He started to turn once again, so Tess asked, "Where are you visiting from?"

"Cleveland. I'm here for a conference."

"Oh, really? What line of work are you in?" Tess was either coming across as a chatty innkeeper or the nosiest woman in Marietta.

"Pet food." He grinned. "I'm in sales for a new brand of dog food that's all-natural. No chemicals, hormones, or antibiotics in any of our products."

"That sounds great," Tess said. "We don't have any pets here, sadly, but my late husband and I used to have dogs, and we had no idea what was in their food. I'm sure you're finding that people care about things like that these days."

He laughed. "Well, if they don't, I try to get them to care about it." He turned to the café again. "If you'll excuse me, I need to get going. I have an early meeting, and I'm hoping to get something to eat first."

"Of course." Tess gestured toward the café, and he walked over and sat down at one of the tables on the far side of the room from Sharon and Jack. Taylor came up and took his order, and Tess watched for a moment while Isaiah pulled an iPad out of his briefcase and started reading something on the screen.

She turned back to her own iPad on the check-in desk. She had said they would look into their guests, so she decided to start with Isaiah. She looked up the Marietta Chamber of Commerce site and tried to figure out if there was a way to find out which conventions were being held where. There didn't seem to be a public listing, but maybe she could find—

"How's it going?"

Tess looked up and saw LuAnn standing in front of the desk.

"Quiet so far." She nodded in the direction of the café. "Just the Willards and Mr. Sellers. He's off to a business meeting."

"Did you talk to him?" LuAnn asked under her breath.

Tess nodded, but she didn't want to get into it within earshot of their guest. "I'll fill you in later."

"All right then. Janice is upstairs cleaning the common area on our floor. I'm going to make a shopping list of things to get when I go to the store today, and then I'm going to head in to help Winnie. Is there anything you can think of that we need?"

"Could you pick up some more of those dryer sheets?" Laundry was a never-ending chore at the inn, but they'd found some dryer sheets they liked that gave the sheets a nice, fresh smell.

"I sure can. We need to restock cleaning and laundry supplies in general, so I'll grab a bunch."

"Thank you." Footsteps on the stairs made them both look up. Tess recognized Fiona Howell coming down the steps, trailing her fingertips along the bannister. Fiona was in her early thirties, Tess guessed, and had long brown hair and porcelain skin. LuAnn had checked her in yesterday, and Tess had met her briefly. She was an antiques dealer from Chicago, she said, and she traveled around to scour flea markets and vintage shops for pieces she could fix up and resell in her shop in Wicker Park. They both looked up and smiled as she came down the last few steps.

"Good morning. Did you sleep well?" Tess asked. She really wanted to ask whether Fiona had gotten out of bed to do any nocturnal wandering, but she kept a smile on her face and bit her tongue.

"Very well. This place is so cool." Fiona wore skinny jeans and ankle boots with a leather jacket. She pulled a phone out of her pocket and took a picture of the café area. "Wow. The way the light is coming in through that window is so gorgeous."

Tess nodded, watching carefully. The morning light in this room, which overlooked the river, really was beautiful.

"Do you have anything fun planned for today?" LuAnn asked.

"Just poking around." Fiona stepped away from the desk and to the right of it a few feet and looked into the lounge area. She took pictures of the room—and of the painting, Tess noted—squatting down to get the shot from different angles.

Tess came around the desk and joined Fiona as she aimed her phone at a small writing table and chair. "You've decorated so authentically," Fiona said to her.

"Thank you," Tess said. "That's a Hitchcock."

Fiona turned back, her brow wrinkled. "Like the movies?"

Tess looked at LuAnn, whose eyes were wide. Tess shook her head. "That black chair you just took a picture of." She pointed to the wooden spindle-backed chair with a stenciled design. It was a quintessential example of the distinctive classic American furniture maker's style, though the piece itself was a reproduction. Was that what was throwing her off?

"Oh, right. Of course." She stepped forward and touched the arm of the chair gently. "It's beautiful. Though my taste runs more toward midcentury modern." She zoomed in, took another picture of the chair, and then walked back toward them.

"Well, I'm sure you'll find plenty of that at the Antique and Salvage Mall in town," Tess said. She glanced at LuAnn, and saw that she'd caught it too. Fiona had never heard of Hitchcock furniture. "They always have lots of interesting finds."

"Yes, I'm excited to see what's around. I was planning to start off in Harmar Village. I've heard they have lots of cute shops there. This is such a neat town."

"We do love it," LuAnn said.

"There's so much history here. I love the cobblestone streets and the gorgeous old buildings. And I read that this place used to be a stop on the Underground Railroad."

"That's right." Tess nodded. "The tunnel that ran from the basement to the river is still intact."

"Wow. That's amazing. Could I see it?"

"I'm afraid we can't let guests down there, for safety reasons," LuAnn said. "It's not exactly up to modern safety codes."

"Oh." Fiona looked disappointed by the news. No, more than disappointed, Tess thought. Crestfallen. "Not even a peek?"

"The basement and tunnel really aren't safe for guests to explore without one of us," Tess said. "We wouldn't want anyone to get hurt or stuck down there." After a moment, she added, "Talk about Hitchcock. Can you imagine getting stuck in that tunnel? That's the stuff of nightmares right there."

LuAnn laughed, but Fiona seemed unsure how to respond.

"I meant the movies this time," Tess clarified, and made a stabbing motion with her arm, a reference to the famous shower scene in *Pyscho*. Fiona nodded and smiled uncertainly. Okay. So this one didn't like scary movies. Noted.

"This is a nice piece. Is it original to the inn?" Fiona said, running her hand along a mahogany sideboard with a rosewood inlay. Its curved legs and rounded front panels decorated with carved shells gave it away as Queen Anne style, not the Federal style that would mark any piece made when this building was built.

Tess glanced at LuAnn, who quirked an eyebrow at her. "No, this was a piece I had in my home. We needed some storage in this room, so we're using that for now."

"Well, when you're ready to sell it, give me a call. I could get a nice price for this in my shop."

"Thank you." Tess didn't know what else to say. The sideboard was pretty, but it was a reproduction. It was fifteen years old, at the most. Could Fiona not see that?

There was an awkward pause, and then LuAnn gestured toward the café.

"Are you interested in breakfast? Winnie has made some delicious oatmeal, and we always have eggs and bacon."

"Oh. Not for me, thanks. I never eat breakfast. But I'll grab some coffee."

Tess glanced at LuAnn again. She never understood people who didn't eat breakfast. Weren't they starving? But that must be how the young woman stayed so thin.

"There's plenty of coffee. Enjoy."

She thanked them and headed toward the café's coffee stand, and Tess and LuAnn watched her carefully. Fiona glanced at Isaiah, but he didn't look up, and there was no flicker of recognition on her face. Tess planned to watch Fiona as she made her way through the lobby to see if she checked behind the painting, but just then her cell phone rang. Tess yanked it out of her back pocket and looked down at the screen. Lizzie.

"I have to take this," Tess said. LuAnn waved at her and took Tess's place behind the check-in desk.

Tess whispered her thanks, then stepped out the front door and onto the brick pathway a few paces behind Fiona.

"Hi Lizzie," she said. "How's it going?" A brisk breeze blew off the river, and she pulled her cardigan around herself more tightly. She should have grabbed a jacket. November had brought a distinct chill to the air.

"I'm fine. Crazy as ever. But fine. How are you? How's everything going with the inn?"

"It's going great. Word is starting to spread, and we've got rooms booked through the holidays. We might even be full up during Thanksgiving. So that's good." Tess watched as Fiona walked around the side of the inn toward the parking area and climbed into a small gray car. Was she really planning to haul antiques back to Chicago in that thing? "How are the kids?"

"They're good. Liam fell off the slide at preschool yesterday and scraped his nose, but other than that they're fine."

"Poor thing." Tess pictured his sweet little face and her heart melted. "I hope he's okay."

"There were a few tears, but pretty soon he was chasing his sister around and had forgotten all about it."

"Well, good. I'm glad to hear it. And how are the other two?"

"They're fine. Same as ever, I guess. Henry just wants to give you a hug, and Harper just wants to make you laugh."

"She does, doesn't she?" Tess chuckled. It had been such a delightful surprise when they'd found out that after years of frustration and disappointment, Lizzie would be having not one, not two, but three babies, and Tess loved that they lived close enough that she got to see them regularly.

"Anyway, they're all playing in their room quietly for a moment, which is a minor miracle, so I thought I'd grab the opportunity to give you a call. I'm trying to get the final count for Thanksgiving. Jeff Jr. is going to Kentucky to visit his new girlfriend's family, but I didn't hear whether you're coming or not."

"Oh." Of course Tess would love to join Lizzie and her family for Thanksgiving. But this was the first Lizzie had mentioned it. Truthfully, Tess hadn't been sure whether she would be invited or not, because she knew Michael's parents were coming for the holiday, and Lizzie's table was only so big. And with most of the guest rooms booked over the holiday weekend, Tess wasn't sure how much time she'd have free. But she wanted to come if Lizzie would have her. "I would—I mean, I—"

"If you can't make it, that's totally fine. Maybe better for you, really. It's going to be a full house around here. Michael's older brother is coming now too, along with his wife and kids, so it's just going to be chaos."

Wait. Was Lizzie saying she didn't want Tess to come?

"I'm not sure. I—"

"And aren't you doing that Thanksgiving dinner at the inn?"

"Y-yes. I think so." They had discussed hosting a Thanksgiving meal at the inn for any guests who didn't have family in town. Janice would be spending the holiday with her family, but LuAnn was excited about the idea. They hadn't decided for sure, though, and that didn't automatically mean Tess couldn't go to Lizzie's. Did it? Did Lizzie want her to come? It was sure starting to sound like she didn't.

"It *will* be pretty busy around here," Tess said. A gust of wind rustled the last of the dry leaves that clung to the oaks and sycamores in front of the inn. In a week or so, the leaves would be all gone. There was a crash, followed by a toddler's tears.

"Oh dear. Sorry Mom, I gotta go. So, I won't plan on having you for now, it sounds like."

Tess said, "Okay," because she wasn't sure what else to say, and before she had time to say anything more, Lizzie had hung up.

Tess stood still for a moment, looking down at her phone. Had she heard that wrong? It sure sounded like Lizzie didn't want her to come for Thanksgiving. It seemed like she wasn't *un*invited, exactly, but she didn't exactly feel welcome either. Was that what Lizzie had intended?

Tess shook her head. She had just sort of assumed she'd be welcome to go to Lizzie's, but she realized now that she shouldn't have made that assumption. It wasn't like she'd always done so. Last year, she and Jeff Jr. had gone to visit an aunt who was turning eighty, and a few years before that, right after Jeffrey had passed away and Lizzie was heavily pregnant, they'd skipped Thanksgiving altogether. And she knew Michael's family lived in Massachusetts and didn't come to visit all that often, while she got to see Lizzie and the kids all the time. So it was a big deal for Lizzie to host them, and she was surely stressed about it. But she still hadn't expected to be...well, pushed aside.

Tess took a deep breath. That wasn't what Lizzie had meant, she was sure.

But that was how it felt.

Well, it wasn't as if she didn't have plenty to do around here anyway. She took a deep breath and then let it out slowly. She'd be able to help out with LuAnn's dinner, and that would be on top of all the regular chores they had to do to keep this place running. She probably wouldn't have even had time to go to Lizzie's anyway, now that she thought about it.

She slipped the phone into her pocket and went back inside the inn, pulling the heavy wooden door closed behind her.

Isaiah was gone from the café, but a woman she recognized as Helen Zimmerman, a guest who'd checked in Saturday, was reading the newspaper and eating an omelet. Tess found LuAnn at the check-in desk, writing in a spiral-bound notebook. She recognized it immediately. That was the notebook that LuAnn used to keep track of clues when they were working on a puzzle.

"Sorry about that. It was Lizzie."

LuAnn looked up from the notebook. "It's not a problem. How is she?"

"She's fine." It was true enough, and Tess didn't really feel like going into the whole story right now. "What are you writing?"

"I made some notes on our suspects," LuAnn said. She used the ballpoint pen to point to the name Fiona. Next to her name, LuAnn had written "camera-happy."

"'Camera happy?' What's that about?"

"Didn't you think it was odd that she took so many photos?"

Tess shrugged. "That's what young people do these days. Their whole life is Instagrammed. Let's just hope she's an influencer and that she tags the inn when she posts. That kind of social media attention can exponentially increase bookings if the person has a large enough following."

LuAnn cocked her head. "Can you say that again in English?"

"If she posts good pictures, we get more customers."

"Ah." LuAnn tapped her pen against the page. "Well, I don't know about that, but it seemed a bit over the top to me."

Tess wasn't sure she agreed with that, but there was something that stood out to her. "More importantly, she says she's an antiques dealer, but she doesn't know anything about antiques."

"That *was* odd." LuAnn added *doesn't know antiques* under Fiona's name.

"So what is she really doing here, if she's not here to shop for antiques?"

LuAnn shrugged. "Your guess is as good as mine."

"She's also driving a really small car. Which seems odd if this trip is all about finding pieces to bring back to her shop."

"Maybe she had them shipped?" LuAnn guessed.

"It's possible," Tess said. "But not likely. It would make more sense to drive a larger vehicle."

"Maybe she'll rent one for the return trip?"

"Maybe." But Tess could tell that neither one of them really believed it.

"Okay. So do we think that the antiques shopping is a front for what she's really doing here?"

Tess nodded slowly. "I think it's a possibility. We need to find out more, but maybe."

"Okay. What about Helen?" LuAnn pointed to where she'd made notes about their guest.

It was Tess's turn to shrug. "I can't figure out what she's doing here."

"I thought you said she was moving to the area and was here looking at houses?"

Tess had talked to Helen a bit yesterday morning. She was probably in her late fifties, and Tess didn't have to see her driver's license to know she was from New York. Her accent gave it away, as did the fact that she dressed in very fine wool pants and sweaters. Tess was no expert, but even she had heard of the brand emblazoned across the buttery leather of Helen's purse, and knew it cost a fortune.

"Yes. That's what she said. But I just chatted with her a bit while you were outside, and she said she doesn't have any family in the area, and she's never been here before. So why in the world would she choose to buy a home here?"

"It's a great place to live," Tess said. "Who wouldn't want to live here?"

"And I asked what Realtor she was working with," LuAnn continued. "But she says she doesn't have one. Now why would you not use a Realtor to help you find a home if you're unfamiliar with the area?"

"Maybe she's not sure what she's looking for."

"A good Realtor will help you figure that out," LuAnn said.

"And I suppose you gave her the contact information of a very good Realtor in the area?" Tess winked at LuAnn.

"I did give her Brad's name and number."

Tess nodded. LuAnn could pretend she had no interest in Brad all she wanted, but her eyes gave her away. She lit up when she talked about him.

"Well, good. Hopefully he'll help her find a place that fits the bill. In the meantime, did she say anything about a letter, or a painting, or Mark Twain, or anything?"

"Not a peep. Which doesn't necessarily mean she doesn't know anything."

"Just that we don't know enough about her to say one way or the other if she's involved in all this," Tess said. "So we'll keep an eye on her."

"She did say one thing," LuAnn said.

"What's that?"

"She said the shower in her room is leaking, and she asked how to call our maintenance man to fix it."

Tess glanced over at the woman in the café. Her dark hair had golden highlights that looked just a bit too perfect to be natural.

"Did you tell her that you're the guy to call?"

"I thanked her for letting me know. We'll have to get a plumber out here to take a look at it."

"At least she's stopped calling for room service."

"I didn't mind bringing her a snack the first time. But at some point I had to tell her that room service is generally a feature reserved for larger hotels."

Tess smiled. "I'm glad she took it well. Though it does make me wonder."

"Wonder what?"

"What kind of life she's had. She seems so used to people waiting on her."

LuAnn nodded and then moved down to the next name on the list. "Isaiah Sellers. He seems like a nice guy. Too bad that doesn't mean a thing."

"True enough." Tess glanced at the stairs. "Did he go back up?"

"Out the back door. Said he was hurrying to get to a dog food convention of all things."

"That's what he told me too." Tess pressed the button on the iPad and the screen blinked to life. "I was going to make a few calls to verify whether there's a pet food convention in the area a bit later."

"That's a good idea. Though it seems like such a random thing to make up."

"So we'll see if we can find out more about him," Tess said. "And that just leaves the honeymooners. Lindy? And...Richard is it? Are they still upstairs?"

"Yes, Lindy and Richard Marlowe. In the honeymoon suite."

"They checked in yesterday too. Do we know why they came to Marietta for their honeymoon?"

LuAnn shrugged. "I assumed because it's a charming town to visit, with interesting shops and good food. It's loaded with history and full of nice people to boot."

"But there are lots of interesting towns. Why here, specifically? Why this inn?"

"I don't know. I guess we'll have to ask them when they come down."

Tess added *honeymooners* to LuAnn's list. "Most young couples just starting out need cash."

"True. But so do people buying homes and young families and businessmen and...well, everyone, really."

"So that doesn't exactly help narrow things down."

"Not in my view."

They both looked up as footsteps sounded on the stairs. It was Moses and Sharon again, with Jack trailing behind.

"Headed out?" LuAnn's voice was a bit too chirpy, as if she was trying too hard to sound like everything was normal.

"Yes. Sharon has never seen the area, so I'm going to take her out to see the place where my family lived and show her around town."

"We're gonna see a choo-choo!" Jack shouted as he jumped over the last three steps.

"Shh!" Sharon tried to shush him, but he started singing and hopping around the lobby.

Moses looked toward the picture over the mantel then looked at Tess, the question in his eyes.

She shook her head. "Don't worry," she said. "We'll take care of it."

She prayed that she was right about that.

Chapter Four

While Tess ate a quick bowl of the oatmeal that had been tempting her all morning, LuAnn went into the kitchen to help Winnie get started on the day's soups, and Janice took a load of laundry down to the basement to start the day's chores. They'd agreed that someone should stay in the lobby to keep an eye on whether any of their guests looked behind the painting. So since she was stuck here for the next little while, Tess decided to do a bit of research. The honeymooners still hadn't come downstairs, and Helen had headed out to look at houses—or whatever it was she was up to—so the lobby area was quiet.

The first thing she did was pull up the Chamber of Commerce site she'd found earlier. She was hoping there would be some sort of listing of conventions currently being held in town, but she couldn't find anything like that. However, there was a listing of conference venues, so she decided she would just have to bite the bullet and get on the phone. She started at the top. The first place on the list was a golf club on the outskirts of town. Sometimes Jeffrey's club had rented out their building to conferences, but the front desk at this club assured her there were no conferences booked there at the moment. Actually, now that she thought about it, pet food seemed an unlikely match for a nice golf club like that. Oh well.

The next few venues listed were hotels. One thing she'd taught in her hospitality management courses was that you had to be versatile and use a hotel's space for more than just sleeping, and she knew that conventions, meetings, and weddings were big moneymakers. They hoped to host some events at Wayfarers Inn soon. But the first two hotels she called said they didn't have any pet food meetings. Next, she called the Grande Point Convention Center in Vienna, West Virginia—just a ways down the river. They did a great deal of business in weddings but had no conferences booked for that day, they said.

Tess was starting to believe this was pointless. But she decided to make one last call. A chain hotel out by the highway. She dialed the number, and when a young woman answered, Tess said, "Hi there. I was wondering if you could tell me whether there's a pet food convention going on at your hotel."

"Umm...I think it's a pet store convention actually," the woman said. "But yeah. There's a lot of people here talking about dog food."

Tess wasn't sure how to feel at that news. Elated that the calls had finally paid off. Relieved, because it seemed that Isaiah had been telling the truth. Frustrated, because she wasn't any closer to finding out who had left the note for Moses in the night.

She was getting antsy. All that work, and all she'd done was verify that one guest had told them the truth about one thing. She needed to get up and do something useful. It was earlier than they normally started cleaning the guest rooms—they usually tried to wait until all the guests were awake—but Tess wanted to examine the notepads in the rooms to see if she could learn anything from them, and now, while most of the guests were out of the inn, seemed like a good time. She didn't want to wait too much longer, and was relieved when Janice came up from the basement carrying a basket full of folded sheets and towels.

"That's the first load in and yesterday's linens folded," Janice said, closing the door to the basement behind her.

"Thank you for taking care of that," Tess said. "And if I haven't said it lately, I want you to know LuAnn and I are so happy you've conquered your fear of the basement." She grinned. "And not just because that means you can do the laundry now."

Janice set the basket down and walked over to the check-in desk. "LuAnn tells me you all made a list while I was downstairs."

"We sure did." Tess pulled the notebook from the desk drawer and showed Janice what they'd discussed.

"Hmm." Janice glanced toward the sideboard on the far side of the lobby. "She really thought that was an antique?"

Tess nodded.

"Well, it shouldn't be that hard to find out if she really owns a vintage store. You said she lives in Chicago?"

"She told me the store was in a place called Wicker Park. I assume that's a neighborhood in Chicago, though I don't really know for sure."

"Well then. Why don't I make a few calls?"

"That would be great." Tess stepped out from behind the desk. "Do you want to do that from here while I go up and start cleaning the guest rooms?"

"Well, let's see. Would I rather sit here and research vintage stores in one of America's finest cities, or empty trash cans and clean toilets?" Janice tapped her chin and pretended to ponder the question. "I do love decorating, but I also love the way bleach makes my nose burn..."

"Have fun," Tess called as she moved aside so Janice could sit. The stool creaked as she lowered herself down. "And make sure to keep an eye out for you know what."

"I got it." Janice was already unlocking the iPad when Tess went to the pantry and took out the bucket of cleaning supplies. She also sharpened a pencil in the office and tucked it into her bucket before she took the elevator upstairs. She'd start on the third floor, she decided, where Fiona was staying in Apples and Cinnamon and Helen in Lilac and Sage. She knocked gently on Helen's door, and when there was no answer, unlocked and pushed the door open.

She'd always loved this room, with its bedspread of lavender-colored flowers with light green stems. The walls were painted a creamy white, with a purple and green border, and they'd hung watercolor paintings of a lilac bush in full bloom on the walls. The room, with its windows to the south and the east, got such wonderful light. But when she walked in now, she saw the bed was unmade, and there were clothes strewn everywhere. Goodness—how many clothes had Helen brought? She had only reserved the room for a week, but it looked as if she were planning to move in. The closet had been filled, and there were still sweaters and pants and blouses piled over the back of the desk chair and on top of the suitcase, and what looked like three separate rejected outfits discarded on the bed. Her appearance was so meticulous that Tess hadn't expected this.

Tess gently moved the clothes off the bed—cashmere, if she didn't miss her mark—and draped them over the chair, then she pulled up the sheets and straightened the covers, tucking them in to make hospital corners. Janice, a former Home Ec teacher, had taught her and LuAnn how to perfect bed-making before they'd welcomed their first guests. She wiped down the surfaces in the bathroom and emptied the trash can, which contained only the toilet paper Helen had used to blot her lipstick. She went to the desk and found the notepad with the inn's logo on it. Retrieving the pencil from the cleaning bucket, she held it at a horizontal angle over the page and made wide sweeps with the side of the lead. Tess had seen this trick on one of those BBC mysteries she liked to watch, with the big houses and the mysterious murders and the tea and crumpets. The graphite would reveal any indentation in the paper left by writing on the page above it. But there was nothing. No indentation at all, just smooth gray graphite.

Tess ripped the page off, gathered her supplies, and stepped out of the room. She crossed the hall and walked to Apples and Cinnamon, knocked gently again, and entered when no one answered. This room was meticulously neat. Fiona had made the bed, hung up her clothes, and tucked her suitcase into the bottom of the closet. As Tess wiped down the bathroom, she noticed that even Fiona's toiletries case was zipped closed and tucked into the little nook under the sink. This room had been done in warm rusts and browns and reds, and it felt more appropriate than ever at this time of year. The sycamore along the side of the inn still clung to a few gold and red leaves that showed through the window, adding to the fall feeling.

After Tess had cleaned the room, she went to the desk, where the inn's notepad was lined up squarely next to the phone. She picked up the notepad and rubbed her pencil over it, holding her breath as words began to emerge. *Hawthorne*, she thought the top one said. She kept going. *Irving. Thoreau. Twain. Melville. Stowe.*

Her heart rate sped up when she saw *Twain*. Was it—could this be—?

But she wasn't sure what to make of the rest of it. It was a list of authors; she could see that. But how did they all fit into this mystery? She set the notepad down and took out her phone to see the picture she'd taken of the note that had been slipped under Moses's door. *I have the SLC treasure. Leave a cashier's check for $50,000 in an envelope behind the painting in the lobby and wait for further instructions.*

It didn't even actually mention Mark Twain, she realized now. But it did mention SLC. Surely it couldn't be a coincidence that Twain's name was on a list of authors in this room on the same day they'd learned about the Willard family's Mark Twain treasure. She checked the trash can, but there were no other pages from the notepad—or anything at all—in the room's wastebaskets.

Tess ripped the page from the notepad and tucked it into her pocket, gathered up her supplies, and headed out into the hall. Moses and Sharon were staying in Sunshine and Daisies, and when she pushed open the door, she saw the familiar chaos that indicated a young family was present. There was a toddler-sized blow-up mattress on the floor—they'd offered a cot, but the family had brought their own bed for Jack—as well as a bassinet set up next to the bed for Sadie. There were board books and toy cars scattered across the desk and a package of infant diapers and wipes set up next to a blanket spread out on the floor. She recognized it as a makeshift changing station.

Tess cleaned the room, straightening as she went, and it looked a little more orderly by the time she'd finished. She used her pencil to check the room's notepad, just to be certain, but all her pencil revealed was a ten-digit number. A phone number, no doubt. She punched the number into her phone and found it was the number to make a reservation at the Buckley House, an upscale restaurant in a historic home in town. Tess remembered that the previous guests in this room—a couple in their fifties celebrating their anniversary—had eaten there.

She returned to the hallway and went down to clean Isaiah's room, but she found nothing on his notepad. The door to the honeymoon suite was still closed, and she didn't want to disturb the lovebirds if they were still inside, so she returned to the main floor to get an update. She found Janice behind the desk, looking down at the iPad.

"Any luck?" Tess asked, setting the bucket of supplies down.

"Not a soul has come through here. The honeymooners are still upstairs, and everyone else is out. No one has even glanced at the painting, let alone checked behind it. But I did figure something out," Janice said.

"What's that?" The smell coming out of the kitchen was making Tess's mouth water, and it was still more than an hour until the café opened for lunch. Winnie must be making her chicken noodle soup again. She simmered the chicken for hours, and it filled the whole inn with the most heavenly smell.

"I called all the vintage stores and thrift stores I could find in the Wicker Park area of Chicago, and none of them is owned by a Fiona Howell."

"I guess that's not all that surprising," Tess said.

Janice nodded. "Given what you've told me about her knowledge of antiques, or lack thereof, I do think it's plausible that she gave us a cover story."

"But why?"

That was the question neither one of them could answer.

Chapter Five

Moses and Sharon returned to the inn just after noon, dragging a very tired Jack. Sadie was strapped to Sharon's chest and was letting out soft whimpering cries.

"How was your morning?" Janice asked from behind the check-in desk. Tess was in the office paying bills, but she stepped out when she heard the family return.

"It was great. This town is so beautiful. I can't believe all the history," Sharon said. "And to think, this inn—and Moses's family—was a part of it."

"It is a pretty special place," Tess said.

"I took her to see the patch of land where my great-great-great-grandparents' farm was," Moses said. "The buildings are all gone, and now it's just a field between two housing developments, but still. It's special to our family. My grandparents used to take me to see it whenever we came to visit when I was a kid. Part of the barn still stood then."

"And we saw the church where his grandparents were married," Sharon said. "And his great-grandparents before them."

"Is that the brick one out on Meetinghouse Road?" Janice asked.

Moses nodded.

"That's a gorgeous old building," Janice said. "The congregation still meets there, doesn't it?" Her husband had pastored a church in the area before his death, and she knew a lot about the other churches in the region.

"It does. The doors were open, so we got to walk around inside," Sharon said. "It was so stark and simple and beautiful."

Sadie's whimpering had taken on a more insistent timbre.

"What are you all up to this afternoon?" Tess said.

"I've got to feed this one and get them both down for a nap," Sharon said. She looked around, searching for Jack, who was in the process of attempting to climb up the bricks of the old fireplace.

"Jack," Moses said, his voice stern. The little boy jumped down and came over to his father's side.

"I'll take these guys upstairs," Sharon said. Little Sadie's cries had turned indignant, and Sharon patted her back softly. "I better get this one fed before there's an uprising." She started up the stairs, Jack trudging behind her, and Moses turned to look at the fireplace.

"Did anyone..."

"That was the most attention anyone has paid to the fireplace all day," Tess said, answering the question he hadn't yet asked. Lindy and Richard, the honeymooners, had finally come down about an hour ago, but they had left quickly, without so much as a glance at the fireplace or the picture.

She couldn't read the look on his face. "I've been thinking about what to do about that," he said. "And I came up with an idea."

"What's that?" Tess asked. She and Janice both leaned forward.

"I was thinking I would stick a note in an envelope and put it back there," Moses said. "Saying that I need proof that this person has the treasure."

"That seems reasonable enough to me," Janice said. Her blonde curls bounced as she nodded. "Before you leave any money, you'd want to know they're telling the truth."

"Exactly," he said. "And I was also wondering about something. You all showed me copies of the pages of my great-great-great-grandmother's diary. But you said the originals were nearby?"

"Yes. The original diary is at the Marietta Underground Railroad Museum," Tess said.

"That's near here?"

"It's just a few blocks away. They have wonderful displays on all sorts of interesting topics. The Willard diary is not usually on display, but I bet Maybelline would let you see it if we gave her a heads-up."

"How would we do that?"

"I'll give her a call," Tess said. "Were you hoping to see that today?"

"I was thinking that might be something I could do while the kids are napping," he said.

"That would make sense," Tess agreed. She didn't think Maybelline would respond well to having little Jack climb all over the displays. "How about I give her a call now?"

"That would be wonderful," he said. "Thank you." He ducked his head. "In the meantime, I'd better get some lunch and take it upstairs before Jack tears the room apart."

"You go on up. I'll bring it to you. What would you like?" Tess asked.

A few minutes later, after she'd taken two bowls of chicken noodle soup and a peanut butter and jelly sandwich up to the room, she found herself in the office, waiting on hold for Maybelline Rector to come to the phone. LuAnn appeared in the doorway, tote bags tucked under her arm and a shopping list in her hand. Tess signaled for her to wait.

Finally, Maybelline said into the phone, "Yes?"

"Hi, Maybelline? This is Tess, from Wayfarers Inn."

"Yes. That's what Emma told me." Was Tess imagining it, or could she hear Maybelline tapping her pen against the desk? Well. She wasn't going to make this easy, was she?

"We have a Moses Willard staying with us. He's—"

"Moses Willard? Of the Willard family of Marietta?" The tenor of Maybelline's voice changed completely, her words rising an octave as she spoke.

"That's the one. I think he's Moses the Fifth or something like that." Tess could tell Maybelline was interested to know more, so she rushed on before Maybelline could interrupt her again.

"He would like to see Prudence's diary. We were hoping you might be able to let him take a look."

"When?"

"This afternoon, ideally."

"All right," Maybelline said, and then added with a note of importance, "Of course, most people would need to make an appointment well in advance. It's not easy to just stop what we're doing and let people peruse the valuable items in the collection. But in this case, we can make an exception, considering he's actually from the Willard family."

"Thank you," Tess said. "That's very accommodating of you." It took all she had to keep from teasing the serious woman. Appointments had never been necessary when they'd needed information in the past. "I'm sure he'll really appreciate it."

"I'll see him shortly then. One of you will come along as well?"

"I—" Tess hesitated. What? "Do you need one of us?"

"Anyone could waltz in here and pretend to be him. I'll need one of you to vouch for his identity."

"Oh. Okay." Tess wasn't sure why Maybelline thought there might be hordes of people eager to take a look at the diary today, or why she didn't simply ask for identification when he came into the museum. "Sure."

"Great," Maybelline said. "See you shortly."

"Bye."

Truthfully, Tess was curious to see the old diary as well. She always enjoyed seeing Prudence's handwritten pages. But she was also curious to see if there was some clue they'd missed when they'd looked at the photocopies. Would there be some hint—something that had been too faint to copy—in the original that would tell them what the Twain treasure was?

She set the phone down and stepped out of the office.

"How did it go?" Janice asked, coming into the office.

"Maybelline wants him to come by in a while. She didn't hesitate to give permission once she heard who the guest was."

"She'll no doubt pepper him with questions about his family history," Janice said. "A real living descendant of Prudence and Jason Willard. In Maybelline's world, it doesn't get much better than that."

"No doubt." Tess shrugged. "She also asked that one of us accompany him. Which I was thinking we should do anyway, just to see if there's anything we missed that doesn't show up on the photocopies. I'm happy to go."

"That's a good idea," Janice said. "LuAnn is on her way out to run errands, so why don't I stay here and keep an eye on things." She cast a meaningful glance at the fireplace.

"I won't be gone long," said LuAnn. "And then I'll take a turn keeping watch."

"That sounds good," Tess said. "I'll run upstairs and clean the honeymoon suite while Moses is eating lunch."

"Did you find anything in the other rooms?" LuAnn asked.

"Oh! I almost forgot. Check this out." Tess went back into the office and retrieved the rubbing she'd taken from Fiona's room. She showed it to LuAnn and Janice.

"These are all famous authors," Janice said.

"Famous *American* authors," LuAnn said. "Herman Melville wrote *Moby Dick*. Nathaniel Hawthorne wrote *The Scarlet Letter*. Henry David Thoreau wrote *Walden*. Harriett Beecher Stowe wrote *Uncle Tom's Cabin*, and Washington Irving wrote *The Legend of Sleepy Hollow*."

"And of course Mark Twain wrote *The Adventures of Huckleberry Finn* and *The Adventures of Tom Sawyer*," Tess added.

"Among other things," LuAnn said. "But if Fiona is behind the notes, why would she have a list of authors besides Mark Twain?"

"Maybe the treasure is much bigger than just Mark Twain?" Janice suggested. "Is it possible these other authors might have something to do with the treasure too?"

"I don't know." LuAnn shrugged. "It's hard to believe that all these famous writers could have contributed to the treasure in some way. But then again, the whole idea of a Mark Twain treasure seems crazy to begin with."

"And it seems mighty convenient for this list to show up today with his name on it if there's no connection to the missing treasure," Janice added.

"Which moves Fiona right to the top of the suspect list," Tess said. The others nodded.

"Well, for now, I'll stay here and keep an eye on the lobby," Janice said.

"And I'll run up and clean that last room before taking Moses to see the diary," Tess said. LuAnn held up her shopping list and tote bags and started toward the door.

Tess went upstairs and cleaned the honeymoon suite, which occupied a large room on the second floor. The room was beautiful, with soothing blue walls and a green and blue bedspread. The windows offered views out both the front and the back of the house, and filled the room with light. The couple staying here had kept the room neat, and there was nothing in the trash can and no markings on the notepad on the desk. Tess cleaned the bathroom and came downstairs and had time to grab a bite to eat before Moses came down.

"Ready to check out the museum?" Tess asked when he approached. Janice had filled him in on Maybelline's request that one of them go with him to the museum, and he seemed fine with the idea of Tess accompanying him.

"Just need to do one thing first," he said, pulling something out of his pocket. Tess saw that it was an envelope. She realized it had to be the note he'd said he would leave, the one asking for proof that the treasure existed. He tucked the envelope behind the picture.

"I'll keep an eye on whoever goes past," Janice promised.

Moses thanked her, and then he nodded at Tess and started toward the door.

"Thank you for taking me to see the diary," he said. They stepped through the door, and he closed it softly behind them. The air was chilly, but the day was bright and the sky a beautiful deep blue.

"You're welcome," Tess said. "It's really incredible that it survived, and we're very lucky to have it. It's given us so much information about what life was like while the Underground Railroad was operational. Plus, you just get a sense of who Prudence was, which is really incredible."

Moses smiled. "I'm really excited to see the original."

"It won't be long now," Tess said as they walked to the bluestone sidewalk that curved around the cobblestone street. They passed the Sassy Seamstress, and Tess saw that Wendy had displayed a pretty quilt of golds, greens, and rusts in some kind of swirly pattern in the window. They continued on, and passed brick buildings with colorful awnings and wooden homes covered in clapboard with colorful shutters. They passed McHappy's, where the best donuts in town could be found, Austyn's restaurant, and Morrison's Book Shop.

"This town hasn't changed much from when I visited last," Moses said. "It's still as charming as ever."

"We feel very blessed to be able to live here," Tess said. "So, you're from Cleveland?" She wanted to make conversation, but there was more to her question than that. She wanted to find out how the Willard family had gone from Marietta to there.

"Yes. Born and bred."

"Is your wife from Cleveland too?"

"Yes, we met in tenth grade. High school sweethearts, if you can believe it."

"That's so sweet." Tess smiled, thinking of it.

"It's helpful having her family nearby, especially since my parents are both gone."

"Oh. I'm sorry to hear that." She looked up at him. His dark hair had just a few threads of gray, and there were only the slightest of lines around his eyes. Moses couldn't be older than his midthirties.

"Thanks. Cancer."

"Both of them?" How awful to lose one parent that way, but two?

"Lung cancer for my dad," Moses said, shrugging. "Breast cancer for my mom."

"That's terrible. I'm really sorry."

"Thank you," Moses said. "It was a rough couple of years. We waited to have a family while all of that was going on, and having Jack helped ease the pain some."

"I don't doubt it," Tess said. "Still, it never goes away completely."

"Are your parents gone as well?"

"Oh yes." Tess sighed. "My mom died many years ago. She had juvenile diabetes, and had some complications that did her in. And my dad passed away about six years ago. Heart disease."

"I'm sorry to hear it."

Tess thanked him and walked in silence for a moment, taking in the nearly bare trees in Muskingum Park, and then she said, "They owned a hotel when I was growing up. I suppose I have my parents to thank for teaching me about running an inn."

"Really?"

She nodded. "In Cincinnati. It was a nice hotel for its time, but I always hated it. I had to help clean the rooms and do the laundry, and I thought it was just the worst. But it's where I learned most of what I know about running a hotel. There and hospitality management classes."

"Your parents must have taught you well, because your inn is great."

"Thank you." Tess sometimes couldn't believe she was really running an inn, after complaining about it so much when she was a child. Her parents would laugh if they could see her now. "So, what do you do?"

"I'm a writer."

"Ooh. Interesting. What do you write?"

"Children's books." He shrugged. "It's fun."

"Picture books?" Tess asked. "I have three-year-old grandchildren."

He shook his head. "Pre-teen," he said.

"Well, maybe when they're older," Tess said. "How about your wife?"

"She's pretty busy taking care of the kids," Moses said. "But she also writes a blog about her life and motherhood."

"Interesting."

"She's developed quite a steady following. And she's always looking for content. She's always taking pictures of whatever she's doing so she can post about it."

"That sounds really interesting."

"She enjoys it."

They stopped at the corner to allow a car to pass, and then they started again. Tess pointed to a brick building on the far corner. It was the Quaker meetinghouse. She'd never been inside. "Is that the church where your grandparents were married?"

"That's the one." Moses nodded. "Sharon and I actually considered having our wedding there as well, but we decided to have it in Cleveland at our church instead so more of her family could make it. But it sure is beautiful."

"It is." Tess cocked her head. She didn't want to be nosy, but he'd brought it up. "What kind of church do you go to?"

"Another meetinghouse," Moses said. "We're Quakers."

"Wait. Really?"

"Really." Moses laughed.

"But you don't... look..." Tess trailed off. She realized she had no idea what a Quaker was like, though she pictured the guy from the oatmeal box.

"I don't look like I drive a buggy?" Moses laughed again.

Tess nodded sheepishly.

"I know. A lot of people think being Quaker is like being Amish or something similar. But it's not like that at all. We don't drive buggies, and I almost never call people 'thee.'"

Tess laughed.

"We're just a church that believes in the Bible and believes that God speaks to all of us," Moses said.

"But aren't there, like, no pastors or something?"

"Some branches don't have pastors. Anyone can speak at those meetings. But most Quaker churches, including ours, are much like any other Christian church service. You might not even know the difference. But we're also strongly influenced by our beliefs in pacifism, social equality, and simplicity, just like our ancestors."

"Fascinating." Tess had known Quakers were instrumental in the Underground Railroad and in the abolition of slavery in general, but she hadn't really thought much about why. And she wasn't sure she'd ever met a real-life Quaker before. "How did you choose that faith?"

Moses shrugged. "I don't know that I chose it so much as it chose me. It's how I was raised. As you must know, my ancestors were Quakers, and it's the faith tradition that's been passed down through my family. And I've always loved its emphasis on commitment to social justice issues. Jesus talked about protecting the vulnerable, and that's what we try to do as well."

"That's really wonderful." His face came alive as he talked about his faith, and Tess could see that it was deeply held and important to him. It was wonderful to see. She also thought how delighted Prudence would be to know that her faith had been passed down through the generations of her family.

"The museum is just up here," she said, pointing to the brick building with large plate glass windows. *Marietta Underground Railroad Museum* was written in gold lettering on the front window. She pushed open the door, which creaked on its hinges, and stepped into the small vestibule. Wide pine floors, dented and scarred from years of use, ran the length of the space, and the high ceiling and exposed brick on the west wall made the room feel expansive and historic. Tess saw that the display showcasing the history of shipping on the Ohio River was still on display in the gallery just off to the right.

"Welcome to the museum." Emma Putnam emerged from a hallway that led to the back of the museum and greeted them. Emma worked at Antoinette's Closet, a vintage clothing store in town, and she volunteered here a couple of days a week. "You're here to see the Willard diary, right?"

"That's right." Moses stepped forward and held out his hand. "I'm Moses Willard."

"It's wonderful to meet you. I'm Emma. It's such an honor to meet an actual member of the Willard family." She shook his hand and gestured for them to follow her to the back. "Maybelline got the diary out and is waiting back here."

Their footsteps echoed as they walked down the hallway and into the room Tess recognized as Maybelline's office. While the rest of the museum was immaculate, sparsely decorated with white walls and simple displays, Maybelline's office was piled with papers and stacks of books. The room was stuffy, and the faint odor of salami hung in the air.

"Hello there." Maybelline stood as they walked into the office. "Have a seat." She gestured toward a round table in the corner of the office. It was the one space in the room that had been cleared off, and the old diary had been laid in the center of the table. Tess recognized the dusty leather cover and the broken binding immediately.

"Oh wow." Moses let out a breath as he saw it. "That's really it, isn't it?"

"That's really it." Maybelline gestured for them to sit down, and Moses slowly lowered himself into one of the padded chairs. Tess sat down next to him. Moses started to reach for the diary, but Maybelline let out a high-pitched noise, somewhere between a shriek and a wail, and he pulled his hands back.

"Wait! I was just getting you some gloves," Maybelline said. She opened one of the cabinets in her office and pulled out a stack of white cotton gloves. "The oils in your hands would ruin the delicate pages."

He obediently took a set of gloves, as did Tess, and Maybelline took a third set and sat down in the third chair, while Emma disappeared back into the hallway.

"This was really my great-great-great-grandmother's?" Moses asked.

Maybelline nodded. "Tess, Janice, and LuAnn found it in the inn when they started renovating. It's really quite a find. It's so rare to have a firsthand account from those days at all, but one that details what it was really like to help ferry escaped slaves to freedom?" She shook her head. "This diary is priceless."

"Thank you for letting me see it."

Maybelline gave a nod and very carefully opened the diary to somewhere in the middle.

"This is crazy." Moses leaned close to read the spidery script. The ink had faded and the pages were yellowed and spotted, but the writing was still clear. "It's really her old diary."

He looked down at an entry from 1860:

Sweet Moses has a tooth coming in. He was up for much of the night. We are all exhausted, but there is much to do. A package is expected today.

He turned to another page.

Moses is walking well now, and spent much of the day chasing poor Patience around the yard.

"Patience?" Moses asked.

"That's her pet goose," Maybelline explained.

He laughed and looked at the page again.

The weather has started to turn. I fear we will not have many more warm days left this year. That will make it less comfortable for our friends who are traveling, but will mean fewer people about, so perhaps it will be safer.

Tess looked up from the spidery writing and looked at Moses. She was startled to realize he had tears welling up in his eyes.

"It's really amazing, isn't it?" she said quietly.

"What they did was incredible. What they risked..." He shook his head. "To think that they kept doing this, even after the first Moses was born. When I think about my son... I don't know." He wiped his eyes. "Risking my own life would be difficult enough. But risking the life of my child to help people I'd never met..."

He bit down hard on his lower lip, but she could see that his jaw was trembling.

"They were very brave," Maybelline said quietly. Reverently.

"They were faithful to God," Tess added.

Moses kept biting down, but his head moved up and down just a bit.

"The part I was thinking of, where she talks about the gift from their friend, is late in the diary." Tess looked at Moses for permission, and then she gently turned the brittle pages until she found the entry she'd been looking for. August 21, 1886. She read the whole entry aloud.

> We had a letter from our correspondent a few weeks ago. It is amazing to think that we have been exchanging letters for more than twenty years now. When we

met, I would never have imagined the blessing his correspondence and his friendship would become. The Lord works in mysterious ways, indeed.

I have seen mention of his work in local newspapers. He seems to have become a person of great fame. Someday maybe I will read his work. But there is so much to do around here, it's hard to imagine finding the time.

Many years ago, he promised to find a way to thank us. I have never wanted thanks from him or from any man. If my life is pleasing to the Lord, that is all I need. However, in his recent letter, he promised a parcel would be on its way to us shortly. A token, he insisted, for what he learned of many years back. As much as I value our friend, I have to admit I was dreading it. No one must know the truth about what we did before the war. The sooner forgotten, the safer for all involved.

Our acclaimed and esteemed friend's most gracious gift arrived four days ago. What a wonderful treasure! And yet, alas, its very possession brings with it an equal measure of danger.

Tess examined the page, looking carefully for stray marks or hidden messages that hadn't come through in the photocopies. But there was nothing. Prudence's shaky, looping handwriting was harder to read, as the originals lacked the high contrast of the black-and-white copies, but she hadn't missed anything. The entry wasn't any clearer about who the friend was or what the gift had been.

"It could be a reference to Mark Twain. But it might not be," Moses said. "It's so hard to tell."

"Wait. What?" Maybelline's eyes widened. "What's this about Mark Twain?"

Tess looked at Moses. It was his call on how much to reveal here.

"There is reason to believe Mark Twain might have visited my great-great-great-grandparents," Moses said, "and befriended them."

"How would they have met him?" Maybelline asked.

"I have no idea," Moses admitted. "That's part of what I was hoping to find out."

Maybelline was quiet for a moment, and Moses continued. "There is a family legend that he gave something to them. Something of great value. I was hoping this diary would contain some reference that would make it clearer. But it seems from what you've told me that Prudence was exceedingly discreet about that part of her life."

"Mark Twain, huh?" Maybelline sat back in her chair and for a moment, her gaze drifted off. Then she sat up again and pressed her lips together. "It's possible." She pulled the diary closer to her. Then, gently, she began turning the pages until she came to entries from decades before. She skimmed the pages until she found what she was looking for—an entry from July 23, 1863.

This night I was afraid we were found out. A man was staying at the hotel, a man of some notoriety, it turns out, though I didn't realize it until later. All I saw was his shock of dark hair and his mustache. His accent revealed he was from the south. He witnessed something he should not have. I still do not know whether he will hold his tongue or not.

Tess read the words twice, trying to make sense of them. She'd read the entry before, but she hadn't connected it to the later entry about the treasure.

"You think she's referring to Mark Twain here?" Tess asked.

"I don't know. I've always wondered who she meant," Maybelline said. "She's so circumspect throughout the diary that it's impossible to tell what she means in so many places. But I think it's a possibility, if what you say is true."

"There's one problem with this theory." Moses used his finger to point to a line on the page. "Mark Twain's hair was white," he said.

Tess immediately pictured the photographs she'd seen of the author, with bushy white hair, a heavy mustache, and a white suit. "Prudence says here that he had dark hair."

"His hair probably wouldn't have been white in 1863," Maybelline said. "You're thinking of him in the pictures taken decades later."

Tess used her phone and did a search for Mark Twain and saw that Maybelline was right. The first picture that came up showed the author with white hair and a mustache. The line of text next to the photo gave his birthday. "He was born in 1835, so he probably wouldn't have had white hair yet when he met Prudence." She quickly amended, "*If* he met Prudence."

"Would he have been in Ohio at this time, though?" Moses asked. "Wasn't he from, like, Missouri or something?"

"I think he was from Missouri," Maybelline said. "But that right there exhausts my knowledge about Mark Twain, I'm afraid." She sat back in her chair and crossed her hands. "But you know who does know quite a bit about Mark Twain?"

Tess tilted her head and waited for her to go on.

"Margaret Ashworth had a display about Mark Twain some years back at the Historical Society. It was all about Twain's connections to Ohio, if I recall. She might be able to tell you more." She pushed herself up. "I'll see if she can come over now."

Tess was about to argue that it wasn't necessary, but truthfully, she wanted nothing more than to have Margaret come over and answer their questions if she knew anything that could help.

"Margaret?" Maybelline said into the phone. "Tess Wallace is in my office with a Moses Willard." There was a pause while Margaret answered. "Yes. Descended from *that* Moses Willard." Tess pictured the octogenarian Margaret already running down the street to meet him at that news. "They have some questions about Mark Twain."

They waited while Margaret said something, and then Maybelline said goodbye and hung up. "She's on her way. I knew she wouldn't be able to resist."

Moses continued to page through the diary, taking in his ancestor's words in her original handwriting. A few minutes later, they heard footsteps, and then Margaret entered the room. How had she gotten here so fast?

Margaret had gray hair and eyebrows that had been drawn on with a pencil. She was a tiny, stooped woman, but she somehow filled the room.

"Hello." She stepped forward and held out her hand to Moses. "I'm Margaret Ashworth, director of the Washington County Historical Society."

Moses stood and shook her hand. "And I'm Moses Willard the Fifth. It's wonderful to meet you."

Margaret inclined her head, as if acknowledging how wonderful it was to meet her. She glanced at Tess and then at Maybelline with raised eyebrows.

Maybelline pulled out a chair and gestured for Margaret to sit. Margaret gratefully lowered herself down.

"Now," she said, turning to Moses. "You have questions about Mark Twain?"

"Yes," Moses said. "Primarily, we're trying to figure out if he would have come through this area at any point."

"They think he might be referenced in Prudence's journal." Maybelline tapped the journal with her gloved hand, her chin raised. She loved having the artifact in her museum, Tess knew. "In 1863."

Maybelline showed Margaret the passage they thought might have referenced Twain, as well as the later passage about the treasure.

"But we're trying to figure out if there's any way this really could have been Mark Twain," Tess said. "He wasn't from anywhere near here, was he?"

"Ah." Margaret nodded. "I see. Well, here is what I know. Mark Twain—or Samuel Clemens—was from Missouri, but he lived all over the country throughout his life. He passed through the state at various times, giving lectures and speeches. And he came very close to moving to Ohio at one point. He even tried to buy part of the *Cleveland Herald*."

"He did?" Why hadn't Tess paid more attention in history class?

"Yes, but sadly for all of Ohio, his bid was refused, and he ended up moving to Hartford, Connecticut, of all places."

Margaret's tone made it very clear what her feelings about the coastal city were.

"But, if I'm not mistaken—and I rarely am—I think he did spend some time in Ohio around the time of this earlier diary entry."

Tess pulled her phone out and did a quick Google search for the words "Mark Twain Ohio." It turned out Maybelline was right. The author had made some friends who lived in the area, and if the internet was to be believed, he *had* considered relocating here.

"It checks out," she said. Margaret leveled her gaze at Tess, narrowing her eyes. She clearly didn't appreciate Tess fact-checking her.

"But he didn't seem to have any love for the state later in life. Listen to this," Tess said, reading from her phone's screen. "He reportedly said, 'When the end of the world comes, I want to be in Cincinnati, because it's always twenty years behind the times.'"

Moses chuckled, but Maybelline's face remained impassive. Tess slid her phone into her pocket and turned back to the diary.

Margaret cleared her throat. "And of course you know that Twain was a riverboat captain before the war. That makes it entirely plausible that he would have come to this area in the years leading up to it."

Tess thought all this through. It was becoming more feasible to her that Prudence could have met Mark Twain here. "I guess it's a possibility that she's referring to Twain," she said carefully. "But there's not really any way to know for sure, is there?"

"I suppose not," Maybelline admitted.

"But there is one thing that makes me think it could have been him," Margaret said.

"What's that?" Moses asked. Tess could see that he wanted to believe they were right about this.

"Mark Twain was adamantly and outspokenly opposed to slavery," Margaret said.

"Really?" Tess asked.

"Very much so. He spoke out about it regularly," Maybelline said.

"It's there in Huck Finn," Moses added. "Slavery is very much present in that book. Remember Jim?"

Tess hadn't read the book since high school, but she did remember the character of Jim, the runaway slave who helps Huckleberry Finn pilot his raft away from...someone. "Vaguely," she admitted.

"Huck wants to head north, trying to get away from the Widow Douglas, who wants to 'sivilize' him," Maybelline said. "He runs away, then runs into his alcoholic father, and eventually gets away from him, and he and Jim escape together."

"Jim is trying to run away from his owner, Miss Watson, who plans to sell him down the river," Moses said. "They start out heading south along the Mississippi, looking for the fork of the Ohio River, which they will take north to freedom." Moses shook his head. "Twain doesn't mince words when writing about the brutality of slavery. The whole book is written around issues of race and identity, but it's also a fairly scathing commentary on the culture of slavery and Southern society in general."

Tess processed all this. If what he said was right…

"So, then, it wouldn't have been crazy for Mark Twain to have been interested in a stop on the Underground Railroad," she said.

"Or at least, to not turn people in if he came across it." Maybelline carefully turned the pages back to the entry where Prudence referred to the stranger seeing what he shouldn't have.

"If we could prove this was a reference to Twain, it could change everything," she said.

Tess knew Maybelline was thinking about the museum and the acclaim that could come to it if she could prove a connection to the famous author. But Tess's mind was elsewhere, thinking about the Willard family treasure. Was it possible that it really *had* been a gift from Twain?

"This gift he supposedly gave your great-great-great-grandparents," Maybelline said. "What was it?"

"Your guess is as good as mine," Moses said.

That seemed to get Maybelline thinking again. Moses turned back to the diary and read more pages, squinting to make out the script. While he read, Tess thought about the later diary entry. Prudence and their mysterious benefactor—Mark Twain, or whoever it was—had clearly corresponded for many years. Was it possible...?

And then... Prudence had not just mentioned the treasure. She had also mentioned that the gift was dangerous, that its very existence put them at risk. Why would that be? What could Twain—or whoever else—possibly have given them that would be dangerous for them to acknowledge?

They stayed at the museum for a while longer, but when it became clear they'd learned all they could, Moses thanked the two older ladies and stood to go.

As they walked back to the inn, Moses was quiet. Pensive, almost. Tess didn't want to be nosy, but she knew he had just been hit with some big information and he might need help processing it. "How are you feeling about all of this?" she asked as gently as possible.

"It's exciting, mostly," Moses said. He'd pulled a knit cap down on his forehead, and he kept his hands in his pockets. "I mean, who wouldn't want to believe that their ancestors were friends with Mark Twain? That he'd left them a treasure?" He took a few more steps before adding, "It's an intriguing idea, if it's true. But there's not really any way to tell if it is or not, is there? And even if it is true, it doesn't really help since the treasure is gone."

"I guess if you get it back from whoever claims to have it, it would answer all kinds of questions," Tess said.

He nodded. "'Claims to have it' are the operative words. We have no idea if they really do or not."

"I suppose we'll see how they respond to your note."

"I guess so."

Tess pulled her jacket tighter around herself. The smell of woodsmoke came from a fireplace somewhere nearby.

"Even if the stories are true, and the Twain treasure is real, there's one part of all this that doesn't make sense to me," Tess said.

"What's that?"

"Why Prudence seemed to think it would be dangerous to them if anyone knew they had it."

"I was wondering about that too," Moses said. "I figure it must mean it was something very valuable. They were simple farmers. If anyone found out they had something really valuable around, that might put them in danger."

"Maybe." Tess thought that was possible. But something in her gut told her that wasn't the whole story. Something about the way Prudence had phrased it in her diary told her there was something else, some other reason why it was unsafe for them to let anyone know about the treasure they'd gotten from Mark Twain.

But Tess didn't have the slightest idea what it was.

Chapter Six

That evening, Tess, Janice, and LuAnn were gathered in the sitting room on the fourth floor, relaxing after a hearty dinner. LuAnn had been inspired to make a butternut squash lasagna with a nutmeg béchamel sauce, and after the dishes were put away, they were just settling in for the evening.

Moses's note had still been there when they'd come upstairs, and none of them had seen anyone anywhere near the fireplace all evening. They had discussed whether one of them should stay downstairs to monitor the painting and see if anyone checked for Moses's note behind it, but then Janice had a brainstorm. She had a video camera and monitor from when her grandson, Larry, was younger. She set the camera up downstairs so it was hidden and pointed at the fireplace. Anything that happened in the lobby area would be seen and heard on the monitor that they set up on an end table in their living room on the fourth floor.

It was a temporary solution, since the camera didn't record, but it was better than one of them staying downstairs all night. Maybe it was their constant presence that had been keeping the person away, Tess reasoned. From here, they could monitor the scene without being obvious.

Now Tess was trying to decide whether to turn on the television or take out the book she was currently reading. LuAnn sat down on the couch with her own thick book.

"What are you reading?" Tess asked. Janice had spread scraps of fabric out across the table and was using a rotary cutter to cut them into neat squares. A bag from the Sassy Seamstress sat at her feet. Oh dear. Someone had let Janice loose in the quilt store again.

"When I was out running errands this afternoon, I stopped in at the library and picked up a biography of Mark Twain." LuAnn held up the thick book, and Tess saw a photo of the beloved author behind the crinkly plastic cover.

"It looks exhaustive," Janice said.

"It looks exhaust*ing*," Tess added.

LuAnn laughed. "I figured it would make sense to learn more about him to see if it gives us anything else to go on with this mystery."

"To see if he might really have become friendly with Prudence and Jason?"

"I doubt I'll find the answer to that particular question in here," LuAnn said. "And if Margaret said Twain spent time in Ohio, then I believe her. But I thought it was worth checking into anyway." She unfolded a brown and green wool Pendleton blanket that was on the back of the couch and spread it across her lap. She'd set a cup of peppermint tea in a dainty china mug on the side table, and steam rose gently from the surface in delicate wisps.

"And what have you learned?" Janice asked, slicing green and white calico fabric into neat strips.

"I just started reading it this afternoon," LuAnn said. "I'm barely out of his childhood."

"But you peeked. I know you did," Tess said. She grabbed her book, a sweet, romantic story set in Oxford, England, and flopped down on the comfortable chair across from LuAnn.

"I might have looked ahead and skimmed just a bit," LuAnn admitted. "Just to see if anything relevant jumped out at me."

"And did it?" Janice asked.

"Yes and no." She opened the book to a page she'd marked with a sticky note. "My first thought was, maybe there was some connection to steamboats. I knew Mark Twain worked as a riverboat pilot when he was young. That's how he was so familiar with the river Huck and Jim navigate in *Huckleberry Finn*. That was on the Twain test I gave my students every year."

"I knew that from Disneyland," Janice said.

They both turned and stared at her.

"What? That giant riverboat ride that sails around Tom Sawyer Island is named the *Mark Twain*. They tell you all about how Twain got his pilot's license on the recording you hear as the boat goes around."

Tess shrugged. "I guess it must be true, then, if you heard it at Disneyland."

LuAnn laughed. "It is, indeed. And so I figured, maybe he came up this way on one of his riverboats, you know, because of the Sternwheel Festival and all that."

"It's a logical connection," Tess said. "Margaret suggested the same thing."

"Well, then it must be right," LuAnn said with a wry smile. "But I can't find anything to prove that. And then I started thinking, maybe the treasure was something valuable that would have been on a steamboat."

"Like what?" Janice asked. She was now cutting a red fabric sprigged with green holly. She was making a Christmas quilt, Tess surmised.

"I have no idea. I couldn't figure that out," LuAnn said. "And the timing doesn't really work anyway. That diary entry you showed us that mentions the man giving them a treasure was written in 1886. Mark Twain had stopped working on riverboats well before then, when the Civil War halted all traffic on the rivers."

"Well, that's less than helpful," Janice said, but kindly, with a smile.

"Of course it's helpful," Tess said. "Now we know that the treasure is probably *not* a steamboat."

LuAnn tossed a pillow at her. "It would have been hard to steal one of those from a safe."

"True enough," Tess agreed. "I guess we should be thinking of something a bit smaller."

"It did make me start thinking what else it could be, though," LuAnn said. "So I started thinking about what else Mark Twain did over the years. I knew he'd spent some time out in the California gold country. That's where he wrote *The Celebrated Jumping Frog of Calaveras County*."

"The what, now?" Janice cocked her head.

"It was one of his earliest stories. It's based on a story he heard while he was working as a miner. I wondered if the treasure is something like, well, gold he picked up in California?"

"Now *that* would be nice," Tess said. "I guess it's possible."

"But I don't know. While we like to imagine huge chunks of gold lying around in the rivers out in California, I get the sense it was more like a few flakes here and there that miners found. Not enough to really pass along for most of them."

"Plus, wasn't it the people who were already out there in California who got the gold?" Tess asked. "I thought I remember reading that people who came west in the gold rush mostly ended up empty-handed."

"I think that's true," LuAnn said. "But it's still in the realm of possibility, I suppose."

"What else did you learn?" Tess asked.

"He eventually married and settled in Hartford, Connecticut," LuAnn continued.

Tess leaned back in her chair. "Margaret mentioned that."

"I always thought that was such a strange place for him, since I always think of him as a southern writer," LuAnn said.

Tess nodded. "On that, you and Margaret agree."

"Right. He had this gorgeous Victorian home," Janice said. "There was an article about it in one of the design magazines I read. It was quite stunning, as I recall. It's a museum now, isn't it?"

Tess pulled her phone out of her pocket and did a Google image search for "Mark Twain House Hartford."

"Wow. It *is* stunning." She held up the phone so LuAnn could see. It was red brick, with designs worked right into the brickwork. There was a wide porch and elaborate gingerbread trim and turrets and many chimneys. A shot of the interior showed coffered ceilings, lush wallpaper, beautifully upholstered chairs and couches, and thick rugs.

LuAnn stood and took the phone from her to swipe through the images. "I remember I read it's where he wrote some of his best-known works, including *The Adventures of Tom Sawyer* and *The Adventures of Huckleberry Finn,* which was a sequel. And"—she handed the phone back to Tess, sat back down, and flipped to a time line in the front of the biography—"it's where Twain was living in 1886, when the treasure would have been given to Prudence."

"And it says here this house was next door to Harriet Beecher Stowe's home." Tess's eyebrows rose as she read from the screen. "Man, can you imagine what their block parties must have been like?"

LuAnn just shook her head, but Janice piped up, "Which makes sense, given what you told us about his abolitionist views. Maybe he discussed them with her."

"Harriet Beecher Stowe was one of the names on Fiona's list," LuAnn reminded them. "So maybe there is some sort of connection there."

"There could be." LuAnn pointed at Tess's phone. "I was wondering if something from the house itself could have been the treasure."

"It's possible," Tess said. "Like, maybe some object that would now be a valuable antique."

"Possibly. Although whatever it was must have been seen as valuable even back then, remember."

"Wouldn't the most obvious answer be that it was cash?" Janice said. "A large amount of cash?"

"I guess so," Tess said. Now that she said it, it did seem like the most obvious answer. "And I suppose it would be dangerous for them to keep that around, like the diary entry indicates."

"I don't know." Janice shrugged. "And I also don't know whether cash from back then would be worth anything now."

"Why don't we ask our antiques expert? I'm sure Fiona could tell us." Tess was unable to say this with a straight face, and Janice and LuAnn both rolled their eyes.

"Actually, it would be a good test," LuAnn said. "To see if she *can* tell us anything about old money."

Tess pointed to LuAnn. "If she can, I'll eat that book." She was about to say more, but there was a noise from the monitor. Tess was the closest to it. She grabbed it and watched the small screen.

"It's the newlyweds," she said as Lindy and Richard Marlowe stepped into view. Lindy was thin and young, with wheat-colored hair, and Richard was a few years older and tall, with dark hair and eyes. They were holding hands, and she was leaning in toward him as they walked right past the fireplace without a glance and headed up the stairs.

"They didn't even look at it," Tess reported to the others.

"That doesn't mean they won't come back down and check later," LuAnn said.

Tess put the monitor back on the end table. "Yeah, but is one of us going to sit up and watch the monitor all night?"

"I don't think that's a plausible scenario," Janice said. "I know I'm too old to do all-nighters, and I suspect you both are too smart to try pulling one." Tess and LuAnn both nodded. As much as she wanted answers to this mystery, Tess didn't think she had it in her to sit up and gaze at a small screen all night, just in case someone came to take a peek behind the painting.

"Moses volunteered to stay up and watch, but his wife was not fond of that idea," LuAnn said.

"She must be worried about his safety," Janice guessed.

Tess laughed. "Yes, probably that, but also, if my husband had left me alone with a newborn overnight, I would have throttled him."

"He really should rest while he can," LuAnn said.

Janice nodded. "So I thought it might make the most sense to keep the monitor in my room when we go to bed and just turn the volume way up. If anyone goes down to the lobby, the noise should wake me up and I'll be able to see who it is on the screen."

"Are you sure you want to do that?" LuAnn asked. But Tess could see the same relief on her face that she felt.

"It's fine. I did it all the time when Larry was younger, so Stacy could get a full night's sleep." Janice's daughter, Stacy, was a single mom, and Tess knew it had been a huge help to her to have Grandma and Grandpa around when Larry was a baby. "If anything happens, I'll wake you up."

Tess was doubtful. It didn't seem to her that it would make much noise to sneak in the room and take an envelope. "Are you sure you'll hear it if someone goes into the room?"

"I used to wake up if Larry rolled over in his crib. As long as I have the volume turned up, I should hear it."

"Okay," Tess said. "So what do you all think of the newlyweds?"

"Hard to say," LuAnn said. "They seem nice enough, but I haven't really spoken with them much."

"Me neither."

"My money is on Fiona," Janice said. "With that list of authors and posing as an antiques expert, she's the most obvious. She's hiding something, obviously."

Secretly, Tess agreed. But she wanted to keep an open mind and not eliminate other suspects too quickly.

"We'll see what tomorrow brings," she said.

LuAnn settled back and opened her book again. "Hopefully, it will bring us answers to what this Twain treasure is."

"Or at least, just a little closer," Tess added.

The sun's first rays were just starting to peek over the horizon when Tess woke up the next morning. She stepped out of bed and pulled her robe tightly around herself. The day was clear, she could see, but cold. Normally, she would dress and brush her hair and have a cup of coffee before she headed downstairs, but this morning, she was too curious to wait. Janice hadn't woken them, so she supposed there had been no movement downstairs, but still, she was curious to see if the note Moses had left behind the painting had been taken in the night somehow. She needed to check.

She crept down the steps, careful to skip the sections of the staircase that creaked and groaned, and stepped into the lobby a few moments later. Winnie hadn't arrived yet, and the first floor was still. Tess inched forward and peeked behind the painting.

Wait. The envelope should be right—she pulled the painting off the mantel, but she'd seen correctly.

The envelope was gone.

Chapter Seven

July 23, 1863

Prudence's heart pounded in her ears, and her legs had no strength to hold her up. That man had seen. He knew.

He would tell. She had no doubt of that. What she was doing was against the law, and there were large bounties offered for runaway slaves.

This would be the end—not just for the man in front of her, but for Jason, and sweet Moses as well. It was—

No. Prudence shook herself. She couldn't lose control. Not now. Not while there was still a tired, hungry man in front of her. A tired, hungry, hurt man.

"Let's get thee into a room so thee can lie down," she said, willing her voice to reflect a calm she didn't feel. "I'll bring thee some soup, and there's fresh bread and cheese. Would thee like tea as well?"

This may very well be his last night as a free man, and she would certainly be sent to jail straightaway too. But for now, while he was still under her care, she would tend to his needs.

She would do what the Lord had called her to do, and let Him handle the rest.

The man didn't answer, but followed her into one of the small rooms that branched off the hallway. It was plain, with just a mattress on a wooden frame, a small chest of drawers, and a white pitcher and basin. Eunice was sleeping in the room at the far end. Oh dear—would she be caught and sent back too? They had passed her off as a free employee of the hotel for many weeks, but she was now in danger as well.

No sense inviting trouble, she thought. She would just focus on what to do next.

"I will go get the food," she said, "and then I'll be back with some warm water so thee can wash up. Then I'll stitch up that arm."

He nodded, eyeing the room warily.

"Thee are safe here," she said, but even as the words came out of her mouth, she knew that neither of them believed them.

Prudence stepped back into the hallway, the candle casting a weak light against the shadows. She took a deep breath and headed toward the stairs. Before she got to them, though, she heard footsteps on the wooden boards.

Oh no. Was he back? Had he summoned the sheriff already?

Prudence's first thought was to run, but where would she go? And how could she leave Eunice and the newly arrived fugitive down here?

She stood, frozen, as the footsteps rushed down the stairs toward her. It was the man. The same man. He hurried down the steps and met her eyes as soon as he reached the bottom.

"Can I help you, Mr...."

"Clemens." His eyes darted around, searching for what he'd seen before. "Where is he?"

"Where is who?" Prudence tried with everything in her to keep her voice level and calm.

"The man. The..." He shook his head, struggling to find the words. "I mean no harm. I brought this."

That's when Prudence noticed the leather bag under his arm.

"He will need to be stitched. He will be glad for this."

"Sir, you must go back upstairs. The guests are not allowed—"

"Your secret is safe with me, ma'am. I was just looking for some food, and thought—but it doesn't really matter. I came down at the wrong time. Or maybe the right time, depending on how you look at it. I know what I saw, and I think it noble. I want to help."

Prudence leveled her gaze at him. Could she trust this Mr. Clemens? Everything she'd learned, everything she'd been told, screamed at her to admit nothing. She knew nothing of this stranger.

And yet, there was no denying what he'd seen. And there was something in his face that said he was honest, that he came back because he wanted to help.

At any rate, they both knew what he'd seen. It made no difference now if she told him the truth or not. One word to the authorities, and they were doomed.

He pulled the leather bag from under his arm and showed her what was inside. A bottle of brown liquid.

She shook her head. "I will use camphor."

"Camphor will not take away the sting of the needle."

"It is what we use here."

"Why don't you ask him?"

This Mr. Clemens was impetuous. Arrogant. Rude. But it did seem as though he wanted to help.

"I will collect the necessary materials."

The supplies she kept on hand for just this purpose were at the back of the cabinet in the storage room. She stepped around bags of potatoes and stores of yams and retrieved the satchel, then rejoined Mr. Clemens, who waited where she had left him.

"He is in here."

Mr. Clemens followed her into the room where the escaped slave lay on the bed, facing the dingy gray wall. He turned over and sat up. His eyes widened at the sight of the man behind her.

"I need to stitch up thy arm," Prudence said. "This is Mr. Clemens. He is here to help."

She prayed her words were true.

Mr. Clemens stepped forward and pulled the bottle of brown liquid out of his bag. "Brandy will help."

Prudence did not approve of spirits but knew the proven medicinal benefit of brandy. Still, she hesitated until the man on the bed nodded.

Well, then. Mr. Clemens pulled a tin cup out of his bag, poured a good measure of the liquid into it, and handed it over.

Prudence sighed. She still didn't know who this man was or if he could be trusted. But friend or foe, they were now in this together.

Chapter Eight

Janice and LuAnn sat across from Tess at one of the tables in the café, each clutching a cup of coffee.

"I stayed up late, and I checked it before I fell asleep last night," Janice said, gesturing to the monitor in front of her. "The volume was turned way up. The camera was pointed directly at the fireplace. No one could have slipped into the living room and taken that envelope without making enough noise to wake me up."

And yet, someone had. Neither Tess nor LuAnn pointed this out, not wanting to make Janice feel bad, but clearly someone had.

Tess shook her head. "Maybe our suspect is a cat burglar."

"Or maybe the monitor malfunctioned," Janice said.

"It was a good idea," Tess said. She wrapped her hands around her mug, enjoying the warmth.

"Maybe one of us should have slept in here after all," LuAnn said.

Tess took a sip of her coffee. "I don't know if that would have helped. Surely whoever it was would have turned back the moment they saw one of us in the room. They might never have taken the envelope, and then we'd be no closer to finding out who it was than we are right now."

"At least we know for sure that it's one of the guests." LuAnn took a sip from her mug. "I came down and locked up before bed, and I made sure all the doors were secured."

"I saw and heard you do that on the monitor," Janice confirmed.

"I even changed the code on the service door, so we'd know for certain that it wasn't Winnie sneaking in that way," LuAnn said.

"I hope you're going to tell her the new code." Janice laughed.

LuAnn nodded. "I texted it to her this morning."

Tess folded her hands on the table. "So I guess we'll just have to watch carefully and see if we can glean anything from how each of them acts this morning."

"I did learn something interesting about Moses Willard," Janice said. "That's the reason I was up so late. I decided to Google him and see what I could find out, and I ended up down the rabbit hole."

"What did you find out?" Tess lifted her mug again. With each sip, she felt a little more human.

"He's a children's book author."

"Yes, he told me that when we were walking to the Underground Railroad Museum," Tess said.

"Did he mention he's a *New York Times* best-selling author? And that he has a hugely successful series of chapter books?"

"No, he didn't mention that." Tess's eyes widened.

"Have you ever heard of the Englewood Island Adventures series?"

"*That's* him?" Tess couldn't believe it. Even she'd heard of those books. She was excited to read them with the triplets in a few years. The series was a phenomenon, with more than a dozen titles and a movie coming out later this year. It featured a brother and a sister whose parents were detectives. The kids secretly also worked on the mysteries, and they always cracked the cases before their parents did.

"No, that's some other author." LuAnn shook her head. "Isn't that author's name Matt Sherman?"

"That's the name he uses." Janice got up and took the iPad out of the check-in desk drawer and brought it back. She touched the screen and pulled up the website for Matt Sherman. "It's a pen name."

"No way." But sure enough, there was a picture of Moses on the webpage.

"And if you look at his author bio"—Janice tapped on one of the tabs on the screen, and it took her to a page that displayed two paragraphs about the author's life—"it says that Matt Sherman is a pen name. It just doesn't reveal what his real name is."

"That's fascinating," LuAnn said. "I had no idea we had a celebrity right here at our inn."

"I don't know that I'd go that far." Tess smiled at her. "But it is cool to have a famous author here."

"But more importantly, it all makes sense," Janice said.

"What does?" Tess asked.

Janice put the iPad on the table. "His books seem to be selling pretty well."

"I'd say that's an understatement." Tess laughed.

"So he probably has made a lot of money from the books," Janice said.

LuAnn narrowed her eyes at her. "So you're saying he was likely targeted because it's a fair assumption he has money."

So many things were starting to line up now. "He didn't seem fazed by the amount of money the notes were asking for," Tess said, realization dawning. "His questions seemed to be more about whether the person sending the note really had the treasure, not whether he could afford to pay what they were asking."

Janice tapped the tabletop with her knuckles. "Exactly. And now we know why. But also, I think he was targeted because of who he is. A Willard."

Tess frowned. "But you just showed us that he uses a pen name to hide who he is."

"But he's open about the fact that Matt Sherman is a pen name, and it isn't too hard to find out what his real name is. I found a fan site where his real name is openly discussed. And then I read this interview he did a couple of years ago for a British magazine—"

Tess chuckled. "You weren't kidding when you said you went down the rabbit hole."

"No, I really wasn't." Janice picked up the iPad again, pulled up a website, and held the screen so they could see it. "Here the interviewer asked him how he got so interested in mysteries, and he talks about a mystery in his own family, about a treasure given to his great-great-great-grandparents that was stolen and has never been recovered. He says he would love to solve that one someday."

Tess thought about this for a moment. "So someone—one of our guests, presumably—gets ahold of the treasure somehow. They do some research on it, and they read the article connecting this famous author to the treasure. They decide he can probably afford to pay a decent price for it, so they lure him here to make the drop."

Janice rolled her eyes. "'Make the drop'?" A smile tugged at the corner of her mouth.

Tess put a hand on her hip. "You have to admit, it's plausible."

"Yes, it's plausible," Janice said slowly.

Tess said what she figured they were all thinking. "But why drag him here? Why the inn?"

LuAnn threw up her hands. "Who knows how a person like this thinks? I suppose maybe because the seller had done research into Moses's family and realized this place would convince Moses he had the goods."

"Or maybe the treasure has to do with the inn somehow," Janice said.

Tess took another sip from her mug. "But why sell it to Moses at all? If whatever it is really is all that valuable, why not sell it to the highest bidder? Why specifically focus on this one buyer?"

"Maybe it's something that's valuable only to a Willard?" LuAnn shrugged. "I don't think we can answer those questions until we figure out what the treasure is."

"And to figure out what the treasure is, we need to find out who is behind this," Tess said. They all looked at the monitor in front of them, and Janice let out a small sigh.

Just then, the back door was pushed open and they heard footsteps on the wooden floor. LuAnn was sitting the closest, and she craned her neck to see who it was.

"Hey, Winnie," she called.

"Hey, yourself." Winnie crossed the kitchen and appeared in the doorway that led to the café. She wore a heavy parka, and her dark hair was tucked up under a brown knit cap. "How's everybody doing this morning?" She looked around. "You're all up early."

"We're discussing the inn," Tess said, side-stepping the real reason for the conversation.

"I see. A business meeting?"

"You could say that." LuAnn smiled.

"Well, in that case, you could add the garbage to the agenda," Winnie said.

"The garbage?" Janice's face reflected the confusion Tess felt.

"Someone got into the garbage last night," Winnie said. "I saw it as I was coming in. I don't know why or who, but that can't go on."

"Someone? Or something?" LuAnn asked.

"Some*one*, unless something was able to unlatch the lid, stuff a bag in, and squash the lid back on."

"Wait. If the lid was on the trash can, how do you know someone messed with it?" Tess asked.

"When I left yesterday, I took the trash out and set it inside an empty bin," Winnie said. "When I came back this morning, that bag of trash was poking out of the lid, and someone had stuffed another bag of trash underneath it. They tried to squash the lid back on, but it didn't close all the way."

"Show us, please." Tess stood, and the others followed Winnie through the kitchen, out the back door, and down the steps to the small fenced-in area at the back of the house where they kept the garbage cans.

"See?" Winnie pointed at one of the bins, which was overstuffed. "This bag was completely inside that bin when I left yesterday. Unless one of you put another bag underneath it, someone has been getting into your trash."

"It wasn't us," Janice said, and the others shook their heads.

"What's underneath the bag, then?" LuAnn asked.

"I don't know. I didn't open it." Winnie threw her hands up. "Who knows what could be in there."

Tess looked at LuAnn, and LuAnn looked at Janice. Janice shook her head. "No way. Not me."

Tess sighed. "I'll look." She walked over to unhook the handles that kept the lid on the trash can and pulled out the white garbage bag filled with kitchen trash. Underneath was another garbage bag, similar to the ones they used but made of flimsier, thinner plastic. She lifted it out, set it down, untied it, and looked inside. It was filled with papers, cut into long thin strips.

"What in the world?" She bent down to get a better look. "These are bills. Someone's shredded bills."

"Can you read a name on them?" Janice asked. "Whose are they?"

"Not the way they are right now, I can't." She peered inside the bag again. "We would need to dig through this and see if we can figure that out. And we need to, because someone obviously has something they're trying to hide. Why else would they go to the trouble of putting their bag under ours?"

"Let's bring it inside," LuAnn said. She hoisted the bag of shredded papers while Janice put the bag of kitchen trash back into the barrel and Winnie latched it closed. They trooped back inside, where LuAnn put the bag on a kitchen chair.

"I guess there's only one thing to do." Tess looked down at the shredded papers in the bag. They could be reassembled, she thought. It would take forever, but if they sorted through the shreds, they might be able to piece a bill or two back together and see whose name was on them. "Who's ready for an art project?"

Chapter Nine

LuAnn went into the kitchen to help Winnie get breakfast going. Tess was pretty sure she didn't have the patience to work on reassembling the strips of shredded bills, and since Janice was the one who loved crafts, they decided it would be best for her to start piecing the shredded strips of paper back together.

"It will be like piecing a quilt," she'd said brightly, trying to be optimistic about the task in front of her.

"Let us know if your eyes start to cross," Tess had said before settling down at the check-in desk. She hadn't been there very long when Isaiah Sellers came down the stairs, dragging his suitcase behind him. Tess checked his reservation and confirmed that he was set to check out today.

"Heading home?" she asked.

"Yep. The conference ends today, so I'll be getting on the road as soon as I'm done." He was wearing another button-down shirt and tie with gray slacks, and he had his iPad tucked under his arm.

"I hope you've enjoyed your stay."

"Oh yes. This inn is wonderful. I'll be sure to book it again if I come back through town again."

"That's kind. We've loved having you." She studied his face. "Did you sleep well?"

Without hesitation, he answered, "Like a rock. I was out as soon as my head hit the pillow."

"I'm glad to hear it." He sounded genuine, and his face had betrayed no hint of fear or concern at her question.

She pulled up his invoice on the iPad and pressed Print. She heard the printer in the office kick on. "Let me just grab your invoice," she said, and she ducked into the office.

"Has it been a successful conference?" Tess asked as she came back out, invoice in hand.

"Oh sure. I made a couple of good connections, and I think I'll even close a few deals today," he said as he pulled his wallet from his back pocket. "But it'll be good to get home." Tess noticed a gold wedding ring on his finger.

"I bet your wife misses you when you're gone."

"It's hard for her, mostly because the parenting then falls all on her."

"How old are your kids?"

"Six and four. A boy and a girl." He pulled out his phone and unlocked it, then held it up to show the picture on the home screen. "Maddie and Collin."

"Oh wow." Maddie had blonde curls and big blue eyes and Collin had his father's coloring, with brown hair and brown eyes. They were dressed in pastel dress clothes. Easter photos, maybe? "They're adorable."

He thanked her and put the phone back into his pocket. She pushed the invoice across the desk. He opened his wallet and counted out several hundred-dollar bills.

Tess stopped herself just in time from saying "Wow." She took the money and counted it. "If you'll hang on just a moment, I'll go get your change."

She ducked into the office again and unlocked the safe, keeping one eye on Isaiah, and counted out his change. He didn't even glance at the fireplace. He was completely absorbed in something on his phone.

"Here you go." Tess handed over his change, and he tucked it into his wallet. "Will you be eating breakfast this morning?"

"No, I'm going to head out," he said. "Thank you for your hospitality."

"I hope you've enjoyed your stay."

"Absolutely." He put his wallet back into his pocket, slipped his jacket on, and wheeled his suitcase toward the door.

Could he be the one extorting Moses for the Twain treasure? If he was, he was leaving at an odd time. And his excuse for being here had checked out, which was not the case for at least one of the guests they had at the moment. Her gut was telling her he wasn't the one, and logic told her the same thing. She watched as he stepped out the front door and closed it behind him.

Tess sipped her coffee as she went through the inn's email on the iPad. They had a few new bookings for December and January, and one inquiry about a wedding for the spring. And two new reservations for the Thanksgiving dinner at the inn. Her stomach twisted. Was she really supposed to be here instead of with her precious grandchildren and daughter? It was hard to even think about.

She looked up as a movement caught her eye. Moses was coming down the stairs. He looked at Tess, and she nodded. "The envelope you left is gone," she said. "But we didn't see who took it."

She explained what had happened, and Moses didn't seem as upset as she thought he might. "They'll get in touch with me," he said. "I wish I'd seen who it was, but if they really have the treasure, they're not going to go away just yet."

"Please do let us know if you hear anything," Tess said. "And we'll still keep an eye on the spot behind the painting, in case they leave any more notes."

"I'd appreciate it." He stepped into the café and started pouring two cups of coffee. "Sharon is feeding Sadie now, and then we'll all be down for breakfast. But I promised Sharon I'd bring up some coffee in the meantime."

"Smart man." Tess watched as the rich, warm brew filled the ceramic cups. "By the way, Janice figured out who you really are."

He turned and gave her a guilty smile. "Technically, I'm really Moses Willard."

"But you're also Matt Sherman."

"That's my pen name, yes." There was a dimple in his left cheek when he smiled.

"That's phenomenal," Tess said. "My grandkids are too young for your books, but I can't wait for them to read them. Everyone loves them. And I hear they're going to make a movie?"

"Thank you. And yes, the movie is supposed to be out next year. We'll see. From what I understand, things never go the way they're supposed to in Hollywood."

"It's not often we have a famous author here at the inn."

"Well, you just opened. It could still happen someday." He picked up the cups of coffee and grinned at her, then went back up the stairs.

She went to refill her own cup of coffee and asked for an omelet from the kitchen. As she ate it she perused the local paper. There'd been a fire in one of the old warehouse buildings across the river. A break-in at a house outside of town, where the only thing taken was opioid medication. A car crash on Highway 77. Goodness. Why was it all bad news these days?

The stairs creaked, and she looked up to see the newlyweds coming down the stairs.

"Well, hi there," Tess said. "Good morning."

"Good morning." Lindy smiled and skipped down the last two steps. Her new husband nodded his response.

"You're up early today," Tess said. "Did you sleep well?"

"Just great. The room is so beautiful. But we slept in so late yesterday that we felt guilty. We wanted to get a jump on the day."

The bleary look on her husband's face indicated that he might not be quite as enthusiastic about this plan as his wife.

"Coffee," he said, and Lindy laughed and gestured for him to go get a cup.

"Did you have a good time yesterday?" Tess asked.

"Oh yeah. We went to that Antiques and Salvage Mall in town, and we spent hours there. There were so many cool finds."

Once again, the look on Richard's face indicated that he might not have enjoyed the time as much as his wife. He poured coffee into two paper cups.

"Did you enjoy it too, Richard?" Tess asked.

"So many old things," he said.

Tess laughed. He was a good sport about it, anyway.

"I like to go to thrift stores and flea markets to find vintage jewelry and fix it up and sell it through an online shop," Lindy said. "We're headed out to scope out thrift stores today."

"Yay." Richard gave a sarcastic thumbs-up, but smiled as he said it. He may not love thrift stores, but it was clear he loved his wife.

Tess watched her for a moment. Lindy's face was so earnest, so genuine. But did that mean she was telling the truth?

"Have you caught any of the night life here in town?" she asked.

"Oh yes. We went on a cruise down the river last night," Lindy said. "It was so fun."

A cruise down the river was beautiful. But they were so young. Why were they in Marietta? Didn't most young people want to go to Hawaii or Paris or Costa Rica for their honeymoons these days?

"How did you all decide to come here for your honeymoon?" Tess asked.

"It's such a cute old town," Lindy said. "I read about it in a magazine a few years back, and saw the pictures of the sternwheelers, and I just fell in love with the place."

"Well, that plus I'm a grad student," Richard added.

"Right." Lindy's smile didn't diminish. "And I'm training to be a surgical assistant, so we basically have no money. But we have the cutest little apartment on campus, and it's only for a few more years."

"Ah." That solved the not-Paris or Hawaii mystery then. Grad students were famous for making almost nothing.

"What are you studying?" Tess asked Richard.

"Microbiology," he said. He had added milk and sugar to the cups and was busy stirring. "I've got a couple more years to go, and then we hope to go on a real honeymoon."

"Richard!" Lindy nudged him with her elbow. "You can't say this isn't real. This is her hotel. And it's beautiful."

"Thank you." Tess smiled. "But it's perfectly understandable. We do love the inn, but it's no European vacation."

"It's got really great coffee, though," Richard said, putting lids on the two cups. "Thank you for that."

"Of course."

"Ready?" Richard handed a cup to Lindy, then put his hand on her lower back and guided her toward the door.

A twinge of longing twisted inside Tess. She missed Jeffrey. Even after all this time, moments like this surprised her, and she remembered how much she missed him.

She watched the newlyweds go out the door, remembering her own newlywed days. They'd fought bitterly, she and Jeffrey. But they'd loved each other dearly. And they'd had so much fun together. They'd gone to New Orleans on their honeymoon, and they'd relished the old buildings dripping with lacy trim, the spicy food, the soulful jazz. They'd gone to see the

French Quarter and walked around the Garden District. They'd always wanted to go again, always talked about bringing their future children back to see the place, but once the kids arrived, it was harder to find the money and the time to travel. She wished they'd found a way to do more of that. It was so wonderful how Moses and Sharon weren't afraid to bring their kids—

"Hello, Tess."

"Oh. Hi, Brad." When had he come in? "What's going on?"

"I'm here to show one of your guests some houses." Brad Grimes was a Realtor in town and had helped them buy the inn. Tess remembered now that LuAnn was going to put him in touch with Helen, to help her find a home.

"That must be Helen," Tess said. "She called you, then."

"She did indeed." Brad wore a button-down shirt and pressed khakis, and he was looking around the room. Searching for LuAnn, Tess guessed. Those two had something going on. She wasn't sure they knew what yet, but there was a definite spark between them.

"Oh good. She seemed a bit…unfocused in her search."

"Well, I'm happy to show her some houses," Brad said. "Maybe I can help her figure out what she's really looking for."

"I'm so glad," Tess said. "She hasn't come down yet, but I'm sure she will shortly. In the meantime, I think LuAnn wanted to talk to you. Hang on."

Tess speed-walked into the kitchen, where LuAnn was going over the day's recipes with Winnie. "LuAnn, Brad is here."

Tess gestured toward the door with her head.

"Does he need something?" LuAnn looked up from the paper.

"He needs *you*." She gestured toward the café again. "I told him you needed to talk to him."

"You did *what?*" LuAnn frowned at her. "Well, you can just go right back in there and tell him you were mistaken. Tell him I'm busy with Winnie right now."

Winnie grinned. "I think I can handle it from here. You know what they say about too many cooks. Y'all go on and scoot out of my kitchen."

LuAnn grumbled, but Tess could see a tiny upward curve at the corner of her lips.

"You're welcome." Tess took her arm and steered her toward the door. LuAnn smoothed her hair down, straightened her top, and then stepped out into the café area.

"Nice work." Winnie gave Tess a thumbs-up.

Tess smiled and retrieved the cleaning supplies from the pantry. She waited another moment before heading back out into the café where Brad and LuAnn were chatting. She would clean Isaiah's room and then the honeymoon suite, and then hopefully she would be able to run out for a bit. As she was reading the newspaper a little while ago, she'd had an idea, and she was excited to check it out.

The inn was quiet when Tess slipped outside, pulling her wool coat tightly around herself. It was about a ten-minute walk, but she decided not to hop in the car, because the day was clear and the air crisp and refreshing. Tess passed the red-brick Marietta Public Library, perched on a hill that she and her friends had discovered was actually an Indian mound. The building itself had been built more than a hundred years ago and was funded in large part by money from Andrew Carnegie and others of his ilk. Robber barons, she'd always called them. Set back beyond a sprawling green lawn, the elaborately carved white trim made the building appear graceful and stately.

Tess spent plenty of time in the library, but today she was actually headed to the library's satellite building, the Local History and Genealogy Archives on Washington Street. She walked up the steps of the smaller red-brick building, which was flanked by Grecian columns. The original oak floors creaked under her feet as she stepped inside and looked around. LuAnn had been here before and told her that this was where the library's collection of historic newspapers was gathered on microfilm, but Tess had never been inside.

"Hello." A man in his thirties waved from the front counter. "Can I help you find something?" He had dark skin and a wide smile.

"I'm hoping to look through the old newspaper archives on microfilm," Tess said.

"Then you've come to the right place. Have you used our machines before?"

"No, I haven't."

"Come on over here and I'll show you how it works. I'm Danny."

"Tess."

"Follow me." He led her down a hallway and into a small room. "All of our records are stored in here." He gestured to a long row of cabinets with shallow drawers. "What newspaper are you looking for?"

Tess hesitated. She wanted to find out if the break-in at the Willard's clothing store, the one where the treasure had been taken from the safe, would have been reported in the newspapers. She guessed the break-in would be reported—she sincerely hoped it would be—but she wasn't at all sure. Where would be the most logical place to start looking for information about that?

"What was the main newspaper in the area in 1928?" she asked.

"Most likely the *Marietta Daily Journal*," he said. He walked over to a section of the cabinets and tapped the metal. "Maybe the *Register-Leader* if you don't find what you're looking for there."

"Thank you," Tess said.

"Anything in particular you're looking for?"

"A couple I know of owned a clothing store back then. In 1928 there was a robbery there. I'm trying to find out more details about it."

"Hmm." He thought for a minute. "I'm afraid that doesn't ring any bells."

"I guess I'll start at the beginning, then," she said.

She opened the drawer for the *Marietta Daily Journal* from 1921–1934 and selected a small box labeled January–February 1928.

"Let me show you how this works." He helped her take the spool of film out of the box and load it onto the machine. He pressed a button, and the image from the film appeared on the screen. "You can turn this knob to adjust the size and focus, and this one to scroll." The image on the screen was black and white, and much clearer than the old orange-tinted images she'd seen when she'd used microfilm in the past.

"I'm sorry I can't help you find it more easily," he said apologetically. "If you have any other information...?"

Tess sighed. "I'm afraid I don't." The idea of looking through the newspaper for every day of the year was daunting, but if that was what it took, she would do it.

"Well, please let me know if you need any help," he said.

"Thank you." Tess got to work. She scanned the headlines for January 1, 1928. The words on the screen were small and cramped, squished onto the page with very little breathing room and no photographs. She read about political maneuverings and plans for building in the city and excitement over a traveling circus that was coming to town, but saw nothing about a robbery. She moved on to the next days' news.

As she scrolled, she thought about the fact that in the span of three generations—from Prudence to her grandson Moses Jr.—the Willard family had gone from being runaway slaves to business owners. She thought about how Prudence never lived to see it, and how pleased she would have been to know what an amazing feat her grandson had accomplished. Three generations after that, Moses—Moses the Fifth!—was a best-selling author. The family members had worked hard, and had been very fortunate, and Tess knew Prudence would have been so proud.

Tess was getting bleary-eyed and starting to get a headache when she finally came across a headline in April 1928. "Downtown Clothing Store Robbed," the headline read. Tess enlarged the newspaper and read the few lines of text that followed.

Willard's Clothing Store was robbed Tuesday night. Selma Willard, the wife of store owner Moses Willard Jr., was alone in the store closing up for the night when a man wearing a mask came into the shop and pointed a gun at the petrified woman.

At this point, the story broke off, and she was directed to flip to another page to finish the article. Tess scrolled until she found the remainder of the story, then continued reading.

The store, located on the corner of Washington and Seventh in Marietta, was opened just two years ago and has quickly become a trusted source for fine men's and women's fashion. The masked man ordered Mrs. Willard to open and empty the safe in the back of the store. She led him to the safe and opened it, and watched as he cleaned it out. The thief then ran out and escaped before Mrs. Willard could call for the police.

According to Moses Willard, the safe contained several days' worth of cash as well as "an item of great sentimental value." He declined to comment on what said item is, but insisted that they would be very grateful for any information leading to its recovery.

Tess tried to imagine what it must have been like for Selma, alone and terrified when a man came into the store with a gun. She shivered. Selma must have hated opening that safe, knowing what was inside. It had, no doubt, seemed like the safest place to leave the treasure, but watching the object her husband's family had protected and cherished for generations disappear... She couldn't imagine it.

The article didn't say what the object was, though. Tess let out a long breath. She hadn't realized how much she'd been counting on being able to identify the treasure from reading an old newspaper. She'd hoped that at the very least she'd find some more information about its disappearance.

She scrolled to the next day's paper, hoping there would be a follow-up article. Maybe the thief had been caught, she thought. But there was no more information about the theft. She scrolled fruitlessly through a few more days, scanning the headlines, and she was just about to give up when she saw something else that caught her attention.

"Grocery Store Robbed at Gunpoint," the headline read. Tess enlarged the article and read it, feeling a strange sense of déjà vu. According to this article, a man with a bandana tied over most of his face had entered a grocery store in Marietta and demanded the safe be emptied. Police had no leads and no suspects.

Tess read the article again. There were similarities between this robbery and the Willard robbery, but was it the same man? It was impossible to say. Still, Tess started to wonder if there were any more thefts—and if the man had ever been caught. She scrolled through the next six weeks' worth of newspapers and came across three more businesses in Marietta that had been robbed at gunpoint, including a hardware store and a haberdashery. In every case, the intruder had worn a mask or a bandana to obscure his face and had asked for the safe to be emptied. Each time, he had escaped before police arrived.

They had to be connected. The newspaper itself said as much by the fourth robbery, with the headline "Masked Bandit Strikes Again."

In the days following that article, there were pieces reporting on the fear that had struck business owners in town, and one on the lengths some were going to in order to prevent break-ins at their stores. The locksmith in town was cleaning up, apparently, and some business owners were hiring more security to keep watch over their stores and their employees.

But had the thief ever been caught? Tess kept scrolling. She finally stopped when she saw a front-page story from June 1928: "Masked Bandit Apprehended." Tess zoomed in on the story and skimmed it, and quickly gleaned that the police had indeed arrested the man they thought was responsible for the recent spate of robberies in the area. A man by the name of Peter Alexander. There wasn't any more information. Tess looked through the headlines for the next few weeks, but there was nothing else. No follow-up article. No word as to whether he'd been sentenced or whether the items and cash he'd stolen had been returned.

Well, she reasoned, she knew that in at least one case the valuables he'd stolen hadn't been returned. The Twain treasure never had been. But even if she was no closer to finding out where the Twain treasure was—or *what* it was—she did have something she didn't have before: a name.

Peter Alexander, whoever he was, was the last person suspected to have had contact with the Twain treasure.

She didn't have a clue how to figure out what had happened to him, though.

She didn't have a clue, *yet*. But she would find out.

Chapter Ten

On the way back to the inn, Tess went a couple of blocks out of her way and walked down Washington Street, stopping in front of the brick storefront at the corner of Fifth Street. The building had large plate-glass windows and raw brick walls on the first floor, and windows with shutters on the two floors above.

This was it, then. This was the place where the Willard Clothing Store had been. The place where the Twain treasure had last been seen. All these years later, it was a clothing store, selling designer T-shirts and colorful sneakers and accessories that cost more than she'd paid for her first car.

She turned and headed back toward the inn. Her stomach grumbled. She hadn't realized how long she'd spent at the archives. She'd skipped lunch, and she was starving.

"Hi there." LuAnn was sitting at one of the café tables making a list of some kind. "How was your morning?"

"Productive," Tess said. She sniffed. There was no mistaking that smell. "Did Winnie make french onion soup?"

"She sure did." LuAnn wrinkled her nose. "I guess the smell lingers for a while, doesn't it?"

"It smells delicious."

"Oh, goodness. You haven't eaten lunch yet, have you?"

Tess shook her head.

"Go grab some. And then I'll tell you about Fiona. And I want to hear how it went at the archive."

"Fiona?" Tess stopped.

"Get soup," LuAnn insisted. Tess wasn't about to argue. She got herself a large bowl and set a hunk of fresh bread on a plate. She carried both to the table where LuAnn was working. "Oh, and by the way, when you sent me out there to talk with Brad this morning, I had to think of something to say, since you'd told him I wanted to talk to him. So I invited him out to dinner tonight."

"Good for you." Tess winked at her as she set the bowl down on the café table. That had worked out better than she'd imagined it would. She sat down.

"With you and Janice too."

"Oh." Tess took a spoonful of soup. Soft curls of steam rose up off the surface. "Are you sure you want us to be there? Wouldn't you rather go out with just Brad?"

LuAnn tapped her pen against the table. "I know my mind, Tessa Wallace. And despite your best attempts at matchmaking, I know I'm open to getting to know him better, but not more than that."

"Yet."

"Yet," LuAnn agreed. "And I don't want to give him the wrong impression, so I told him we'd all love to take him out to dinner as a way to thank him for helping one of our guests."

"Smooth." Tess ladled the soup into her mouth and swallowed. It was warm and rich and delicious. Of course, she was so hungry anything would have been delicious at this point.

"I thought it was pretty clever, considering how you thrust me into that situation."

Tess wasn't about to apologize for that. Instead, she changed the subject. "So what happened with Fiona?"

"Well. Remember how Janice suggested that the treasure might be cash?"

Tess nodded.

"When Fiona came back a little while ago, I asked her if old money would be worth anything today."

"And what did she say?"

"At first she didn't seem to know what I was talking about at all. I'd said 'antique money,' and she thought I meant cash from, 'like the 1980s or something?'"

"Oh dear."

"I clarified that I meant greenbacks."

"Greenbacks?"

"That was what the bills printed by the treasury in the 1860s were called. She'd never heard the term. But she said it should be worth whatever its face value was."

"What?" Tess had no idea what a greenback would be worth today, but she had a strong suspicion that a $1 bill from the Civil War era would be worth far more than a dollar today.

"It doesn't make any sense," LuAnn agreed.

"Well, I think we were already pretty sure she isn't really an antiques expert," Tess said.

"Right. The question is, what is she really, then? And what is she doing here?"

"And why did she lie about it?" Tess slurped another spoonful of soup. "And why did she make a list of authors?"

"And she asked to see the tunnel again."

"You told her no, right?"

"Of course. You know we can't let guests go down there. It's not safe."

"How did she take it?"

"She was disappointed, that's for sure." LuAnn shrugged. "I guess we have way more questions than answers about Fiona. So we'll keep working on that. Now then. What did you find at the archive?"

"I found a newspaper article that reported on the break-in at the clothing store when the treasure was stolen."

"Really?"

Tess filled LuAnn in on the articles detailing the string of thefts.

"So if we found out what happened to this Peter Alexander, we might be able to figure out what happened to the treasure after it was taken from the safe?" LuAnn asked.

"That's my hope," Tess said. "Of course, it's probably a long shot, but if we could figure out what happened to it, we might be able to figure out whether someone here really has the treasure or not."

"And how they got it," LuAnn said.

"Exactly. Now we just need to figure out how to do that."

"Right," LuAnn sighed.

Never the Twain Shall Meet

Tess looked at the paper in front of LuAnn. "What are you working on?"

"It's a list of dishes to make for our Thanksgiving meal." She turned it so Tess could see what was written on the paper. Turkey. Mashed potatoes with sour cream and roasted garlic. Sweet potato soufflés. Roasted brussels sprouts and braised kale and biscuits and gravy and homemade cranberry sauce. Three kinds of pies.

"Wow. That's quite a list."

"It's an important meal," LuAnn said. "And our first real holiday feast at the inn. The harvest celebration we had was a great success, so I have high hopes for this. I just wish you and Janice could be here."

"Well..." Tess hesitated. She didn't really want to say this. Didn't want it to be true. "Actually, it turns out I may be here for the day after all."

"Really?"

"Well. Lizzie's in-laws are coming into town." She shrugged.

"And...?" LuAnn lifted an eyebrow.

"And she's going to be busy with them." Tess forced herself to smile. "They're...well, they're very different."

"Different how?"

Tess tried to choose her words carefully. "They have a boat."

"And that matters because..."

Tess could see the confusion on LuAnn's face.

"Not like a ski boat. A sailboat. That they sail."

"Got it. They sail their sailboat." LuAnn's face was still screwed up in confusion.

"They vacation in 'the Vineyard.'" She used air quotes. "They use the word *summer* as a verb."

"So you're saying they have money?"

"They're that kind of wholesome, all-American money that you want to hate but can't because they're so generous with it. She's on the board of several great charities. He's always ready to help when someone needs a hand. They're basically perfect."

LuAnn took a deep breath. She let it out slowly and said, "Tess. Your husband managed one of the nicest golf clubs in the state."

Tess shrugged and pushed her bowl away. She wasn't hungry anymore.

"You rubbed elbows with senators. You know which fork to use at a dinner party. You are a consummate hostess. You own *pearls*. You, of all people, can't be intimidated by people like that."

"It was only state senators," Tess said.

LuAnn didn't even bother to respond to that.

"They raised Michael. You love Michael."

"Michael is a good man. They did a good job there," she conceded. "Just one more check in the 'perfect' column."

"Tess."

Tess wouldn't meet her eye. She took a shaky breath and let it out slowly.

"Are you worried that Lizzie is choosing Michael's family over you because she likes them more?"

Tess fought to get her emotions under control. She turned the paper so it was facing LuAnn again. Finally, she said, "All

Never the Twain Shall Meet

I'm saying is that maybe it would be better if I'm here after all. There'll be a lot to do, and Janice will be busy with Stacy and Larry, so it's probably best if I stayed here to help you anyway."

LuAnn cleared her throat. "I would love nothing more than to have you here on Thanksgiving. I would appreciate the help, and I would love your company." She paused. "But."

"But?"

"But I don't think that's what you really want."

Tess sighed. "It's fine. Honestly. I see Lizzie and the kids so much. And Michael's parents hardly ever get any time with them. It's only fair that she spends this holiday with them."

"Tess."

Tess looked up at her friend. LuAnn was gazing at her with something between compassion and frustration on her face.

"I've known you since college. I know when you're saying something you don't believe."

"I don't know what you're—"

"I'm sorry about Thanksgiving. Truly I am. I don't know what's going on in Lizzie's head, but I can only imagine she's feeling completely overwhelmed, with the kids and the job and hosting the holiday. Even then, I can't imagine why she wouldn't want you to come. But it's okay to be disappointed about it."

Tess bit down on her lip. She couldn't make her mouth form words. She didn't—

"Have you talked to Lizzie about it?"

"About Thanksgiving? Yes, I—"

"About how you're feeling."

Tess sighed again. "Not exactly."

"You know what I'm going to say, don't you?"

"You're going to say I should talk to her," Tess said. "Tell her how I feel."

LuAnn didn't understand that it wasn't that simple. LuAnn didn't have children. She couldn't possibly understand the complex emotional wrangling that was part and parcel of raising a daughter. And things had been extra difficult for Lizzie as she'd wrestled through the issues of identity and family in her teenage years. In Tess's mind, Lizzie was her daughter, full stop, just as Jeff Jr. was her son. Just as if she'd been born to Tess. But there had been a period when Lizzie had truly struggled with feelings of abandonment and the desire to know where she came from. She'd sought answers and not liked what she'd found. After she'd met her birth mother, and seen the kind of life she'd been spared, much of her struggle had eased, but those years had been so tough, for all of them. Now, even all these years later, Tess was reluctant to ask any questions about family and inclusion that would bring all that up again.

"We'll see," she simply said.

LuAnn wanted to say more. It was written all over her face. But she pursed her lips and straightened the papers in front of her. "Do you think salted caramel apple pie or regular apple pie?" she asked. "I always like to try something new, but I know so many people just like to stick with tradition on the holidays." The attempt to change the subject was blatantly obvious, and Tess loved her for it.

"Both," Tess said, and LuAnn's laughter cut the tension.

"Noted. And I'm guessing you're casting your vote for both traditional pecan and black-bottom pecan then?"

"What's black bottom?"

"You layer chocolate in the crust before the rest of the filling goes in."

"Definitely black-bottom."

LuAnn laughed and made a note on her paper, and Tess started to push herself up when a noise on the stairs made them both turn.

Someone was coming down, and quickly. Moses spotted them as soon as he appeared at the bottom of the stairs. He held something in his hand. "Look at this."

They both jumped up and rushed to where he was standing. As Tess got closer, she saw he was holding a cell phone.

"I just got this text."

Tess took the phone from his hand, and LuAnn leaned in and peered down at the screen. On it was a photograph of a letter, handwritten on yellowed paper, stained in places. It looked old. Really old. She zoomed in to read it.

Prudence and Jason,

I suspect this note will come a little out of the blue after all this time, but I hope it won't be unwelcome. I have enjoyed your letters over the years, but I am afraid I did not have merely friendship in mind when I wrote to you initially. As you might remember, I promised, all those years ago, to find a way to thank you for what you've done. I have never forgotten the courage you displayed the night I first saw you at Riverfront House—courage that I myself, despite my best intentions and deepest hopes, have never been able to match. You have done so much good for so many, and now, I hope I can do some good for you. A parcel from me should arrive shortly. I hope you will accept it as a token of thanks for all you have done to right the wrongs of this great nation. Do with it what you will, with my full permission and support. It would, as you might imagine, fetch a fair price. You own it now, and all that results from it. Please accept this gift, with my unending thanks.

                         Samuel Langhorne Clemens

"Is this for real?" LuAnn asked.

"I don't know," Moses said. "But it sure looks like it."

"You asked for proof that the person sending the notes had the treasure," Tess said.

Moses nodded. "I guess we have our proof."

Chapter Eleven

July 24, 1863

Prudence was carrying a load of towels to the basin in the wash house when Mr. Clemens emerged from the Riverfront House and followed her across the yard.

"Mrs...."

He waited for her to fill in her last name. Today he wore a light linen suit over a blue silk vest, though he'd forgone the tie, a small concession to the stiflingly humid summer day.

Even now, after all he'd seen last night, and all he'd done to help, she hesitated.

"Willard," she finally said.

"Mrs. Willard," he said. "May I speak with you?"

She looked around the yard. There was no one in sight, but there were eyes everywhere. They were not safe here. It would not do to even be seen standing here talking to this man.

"Come," she said. She led him inside the small wooden structure at the back of the yard. The strong smell of lye burned her nose as they stepped inside. She set the armload of towels into a basket.

Basins of tepid soapy water stood on the table, with two washboards nearby. The basins would need to be emptied and refilled from the pump in the yard. Laundry was the most hated of chores around the inn, with the harsh soaps and the strong smells and the heavy labor of hauling water, but Prudence enjoyed the peace she found out here in the wash house.

"I wanted to apologize for coming upon what I was not meant to see last night."

"There is no need for apologies."

Mr. Clemens watched her for a moment, and then nodded and continued. "I was hungry. I was working on a story and had been so caught up in it that I missed dinner. I was hoping to find someone who could get me something to eat. And I found something else entirely."

Prudence did not answer. The less said, the better.

"I meant it when I said what you are doing is noble," Mr. Clemens said. "This is not the first time you have harbored an escapee."

"I cannot speak of this," Prudence said.

"No, of course not," Mr. Clemens said, shaking his head. "Nonetheless, I want to know more. I had heard rumors, of course, that this sort of thing happened. But I did not know for sure. I have not yet met anyone in my travels brave enough to actually do what so many wish they could."

"It is not bravery," Prudence said. "It is only what my faith impels me to do. I believe God created all people equal, and I cannot stand by and do nothing as our nation supports a system that treats men, women, and children as nothing more than livestock."

"Quite right." He nodded. "I grew up in Missouri, and witnessed the horrors of slavery firsthand. The institution is an abomination, and it needs to be outlawed."

Prudence nodded but didn't speak. She knew only too well the horrors of slavery, but it would not do to tell him her own personal history. Speaking of this at all was already far too dangerous.

"I must get to work." She ducked her head, hoping he would get the message.

"How many have you helped?"

"I am sorry, Mr. Clemens. I have much to do."

"Where do they go from here? What path to get to Canada?"

"The laundry will not wait."

"How can I help?"

Prudence stopped, thought for a moment. She knew what he was asking, but he could not possibly think he could really help in that way. "You can dump this water for me," she said instead. She indicated the basin on the table.

He hesitated.

"I will do as you ask. But I meant with your...guest."

"Mr. Clemens." Prudence did not intend for the words to come out sharply, but they did. "This very conversation puts me, my family, and everyone else involved at great risk. If thee wants to help, the best thing thee can do is stop asking questions. Forget everything thee saw last night and never speak of it again."

Mr. Clemens watched her for a moment. He pulled at the end of his mustache. He did not want to accept her answer, that was clear. But at last, something in his face changed, and he seemed to make some sort of decision. Then he nodded.

"As you wish."

He turned and walked out of the small room. She watched him make his way across the lawn toward the inn. His gait was untroubled, his strides long.

His words had been beautiful. But could he be trusted?

His actions the night before had seemed well-intentioned. But were they?

She did not know. There were many who would pay dearly to know the route the escapees took to get north, and how many passed through these tunnels. Was this Mr. Clemens truly asking to find out how he could help? Or was he probing to find out as much as he could, hoping to sell the information to the highest bidder?

She did not know. All she knew was that he knew too much.

Chapter Twelve

Tess called Janice down from the fourth floor to see the text on Moses's phone. She was as shocked as they had been, and while they were all trying to figure out how Moses should respond, Sharon came down with the kids. Baby Sadie slept against her chest, while Jack rolled a Matchbox car over the furniture. After a lengthy discussion, Moses replied to the text, asking whoever sent the picture for next steps. They all waited, but there was no response.

"We have to trace the number the text came from," Tess said. "If we figure out who owns the phone that sent it, we'll know who has the treasure."

"That's a good idea," Moses said. "But it says it came from a restricted number."

"Hmm." Tess thought for a moment. "Still, there has to be a way to trace it."

"Maybe Chief Mayfield could trace it," Janice said. "Which returns us to the question we asked yesterday morning—do you want to get the police involved? This seems like something they would want to know about. Someone knows they have something that belongs to you and they're demanding a ransom for it."

Moses looked at Sharon, who gave a little shrug. "Like I said before, it's your call," she said. Tess watched her. Sharon was soft-spoken, but it was obvious she and Moses were equal partners in this marriage.

Moses considered for a moment longer. "I've thought about this a lot, and if there's any chance of getting that family heirloom back, I want to make it happen. I'm afraid that bringing in the police will scare this person away, and then it could be lost for good."

Tess glanced at Janice, and then at LuAnn. They had to honor his desire, she thought. But that didn't mean they had to like it.

"What if we didn't bring the police in officially?" Tess said. She'd had an idea, and as she turned it over in her mind, she realized it might work. "What if we just had them trace the number without really getting into why we wanted to know whose number it was?"

"How can we do that?" Janice asked.

"One of Jeffrey's good friends was the police chief out in Stow," Tess said. "He's kept in touch with me, and he was such a big help after Jeffrey passed away. He's always said if I needed anything, I shouldn't hesitate to ask."

A smile spread across LuAnn's face. "You'd ask him to trace this phone number?"

"If that's all right with you both." She looked at Moses and Sharon.

"That sounds like a good plan." Sharon glanced at Jack, who was now running his car over the legs of the piano.

"As long as you don't tell him what's going on, that's fine with me," Moses said.

"I'll give him a call." She promised to keep them updated on what she found out, and Moses and Sharon went out with the kids to do some shopping before dinner.

Janice went downstairs to work on the never-ending laundry, while LuAnn went upstairs to rest for a bit. Tess went into the office and pulled up Kent Gavin's phone number on her cell. She took a deep breath and pressed Call, and then waited while it rang.

"Kent Gavin."

Tess recognized the deep voice immediately. He'd sung bass in their church's choir for years.

"Hi, Kent. This is Tess Wallace."

"Tess. How are you?"

"I'm fine. Busy, but good."

"Busy?"

Tess realized she hadn't spoken to Kent since they'd bought the inn earlier this year. "Oh goodness. I have a lot to catch you up on," she said. She told Kent all about the inn and their adventures and then asked what he was up to.

"I'm retiring next spring," Kent said. "I'm looking forward to spending my days puttering around the house and playing golf every chance I get."

"But you're still currently the police chief?" Tess asked.

"I am indeed. What's the matter? Are you in trouble?"

She wanted to laugh at the concern in his voice. She knew that if she said she was in trouble, he'd get in the car right now to come help her. He'd been that kind of friend to Jeffrey.

"No, nothing like that," Tess said, and then she told him what she hoped he could do for her.

"Well, I can try," he said. "I'll need to get access to your guest's phone records to do that. And unfortunately, I can't do that unless he requests it. Can you give him my information and have him give me a call? Then I'll see what I can do."

"Thank you so much," Tess said. She promised to have Moses call him as soon as she could.

"Tess..."

He hesitated.

"Yes?"

"Are you sure this is something you should be involved in? This all sounds a bit...well, it seems like maybe you're getting mixed up with people you don't want to get mixed up with."

Tess laughed. In the time since they'd bought the inn, she'd had plenty of run-ins with people she didn't really want to be mixed up with.

"I'll be safe," she said.

"All right," he said. She could hear the reluctance in his voice. "I trust you know what you're doing." His tone indicated the exact opposite, but it didn't matter. He was going to help her.

"I appreciate it," she said.

After she hung up, Tess spent a few moments straightening up the lobby, running a dustcloth over the furniture and fanning the magazines. As she worked, her mind kept drifting back to the note Samuel Clemens had sent to Prudence and Jason. What had he sent them a few days later? Tess had printed out a copy of the photo, and she'd read it several times, trying to make sense of it. "Do with it what you will, with my full permission and support." Permission to do what? What kind of support? What in the world did he mean when he wrote, "You own it now, and all that results from it"?

He'd told them that whatever it was would fetch a fair price, but it sure didn't sound like he'd sent them a hunk of gold from the California mines. What could it be? She hadn't come up with any plausible answers by the time Brad brought Helen back to the inn that evening.

"How did it go?" Tess asked as they stepped inside.

"Oh, we saw some wonderful houses today," Helen said. "Brad showed me so many great places, I don't even know where to start."

Helen looked radiant, exuberant. Brad, following just a step behind, looked a little shell-shocked.

"Well, that's good news." Tess couldn't imagine how Helen had teetered around on those high-heeled boots all day. She looked great, with the finely-spun wool sweater and the pencil skirt, but it didn't seem very practical for house shopping.

"Yes. And he's got some more showings lined up for tomorrow too," Helen said. "I'm sure we're going to find the perfect house soon."

Brad nodded, keeping a smile on his face, but his eyes told a different story.

"Oh, and I have some clothes that need to be dry-cleaned," Helen said. "Can you send someone up to get them?"

Tess tilted her head. She ran the words back through her head to make sure she'd heard correctly.

"I'm afraid we don't—"

"I'll be right up to get them," Janice said, coming up from the basement. Tess widened her eyes at Janice, but Janice simply smiled placidly at their guest.

"Thank you." Helen climbed up the stairs. When they heard her get to her room and shut the door behind her, Tess turned to Janice.

"Did I miss something? Since when do we dry-clean?"

Janice shrugged. "She seems kind of clueless about how this all works. I figured we could drop it off at the place down the street and pick it up for her. We'll add the charge to her bill."

"She's being pretty demanding." Tess could feel her indignation rising.

"I think it's more that she doesn't realize this isn't a four-star resort," Janice said. "I don't think she's being intentionally rude. She's just oblivious."

"Oh boy. Have I got stories," Brad said.

"Please, tell us everything over dinner," Tess said. "I can't wait to hear this."

"All I'm saying is, what does it hurt us to go the extra mile for her?" Janice asked. "Wasn't the whole point of this inn to have it be a place to minister to our guests?"

Tess raised her eyebrows at her. "She might very well be the one trying to sell the Twain treasure. What if she's the one trying to extort money out of Moses?"

"Then it's even more important to keep her happy," Janice said. "Now, I'm going to go up and get her clothes, and I'll tell LuAnn that Brad's here. Are you both ready to head out to dinner? Winnie said she'll stay and hold down the fort until we get back."

"That sounds great," Brad said.

Tess started for the stairs. "Let me just freshen up."

A little while later, the four of them were seated at a table at Over The Moon Pizza, a family-run pizzeria just a few blocks from the inn. The menu was written on a chalkboard on one wall, and the other wall was a charming brick. After a few moments of discussion, they agreed to split a pepperoni and mushroom pie, and then LuAnn asked Brad to tell them about his day with Helen.

"She's...a nice person," Brad said. He used his straw to stir the ice in his Coke.

"But...?" Tess was pleased to see that, despite LuAnn's insistence that she wasn't ready for anything more than friendship from Brad, she'd changed into a flattering flowy top in a striking peacock blue-green that set off her eyes and had even put on a touch of subtle eye makeup.

"I don't know." He took a sip from his straw and thought for a moment before he went on. "I can't figure her out, honestly."

"Go on," Janice urged him.

"She doesn't seem to know what she wants."

"Do any of us really know what we want?" Tess said.

Brad gave a half-hearted chuckle, but the others just ignored her attempt at a joke.

"I'm not talking about in life. We're not dealing with existential questions here. I just want to know, does she want a house or a condo? In the city or with some land? Pretty basic stuff."

"She didn't know any of the answers?"

Brad shook his head. "She said she was 'open.' And then she told me her budget, which was a little lower than what I was expecting, to be perfectly honest, based on the image she projects."

"You mean the clothes and the hair and the general sense she gives off that everyone works for her?" Tess said.

"Be nice," Janice said. She pushed her straw out of its paper wrapper. She'd made a detour on the way to Over the Moon to drop Helen's clothes off at the dry cleaner.

"Yes. Well." Brad coughed. "In any case, she said she wanted a home with historic charm and character, so I started off by showing her some homes in her budget. They were modest homes, but in good neighborhoods and with more than enough space for one person."

"Let me guess. She didn't like them?" Tess asked.

"She asked if we could look at something a bit more 'upscale.' That was the word she used. So I took her to see some bigger houses, and she seemed to really like those. There was one on the same block as Aunt Thelma and Aunt Irene's home that she fell in love with."

"Can she afford one of those?" Tess was pretty sure the houses on that block wouldn't fit into a modest budget.

"Not unless she's expecting some money to come in soon," he said. Tess met Janice's eye, and then LuAnn's.

"Then she wondered if I could show her something a little more 'farm-y.'"

"'Farm-y?'" Janice wrinkled her nose. "What did you show her?"

"A farm." He shrugged. "The old Jenkins farm out on Route 16 is for sale. She thought it was charming."

"It's hard to imagine Helen as a farmer," Tess said.

"I thought so as well. I asked what kinds of crops she was interested in raising, and she said she loved baby goats."

"What about grown-up goats?" Janice asked.

He shrugged again. "She only mentioned babies."

Tess tried to imagine Helen, with her cashmere and her high-heeled boots, mucking out a stable or driving a John Deere. She couldn't see it. She knew many city people had a fantasy of moving to the country and playing farmer, but she couldn't imagine Helen doing it on her own.

"I think she's well-intentioned," Brad said. "She just seems to be used to a high-end lifestyle, and has no idea how much things really cost."

"That lines up with what we've seen so far," Janice said.

"Do you have any sense of what kind of house she might end up settling on?" LuAnn asked.

Brad picked up his glass and took a sip, then he set it down and shook his head. "Truthfully? I'm not sure she'll end up buying a house here."

"Why do you say that?" Tess asked.

He cleared his throat. "This all stays within the cone of silence, right?"

"Absolutely. Cone of silence," LuAnn said.

"Well, I asked her why she was looking to move to this area, and she didn't really have a good answer."

"It's a beautiful place to live," Janice said.

"Of course it is. But she's spent her whole life in New York City. She doesn't have any family here. She's never even been to this area before."

"She's never been here before?" Tess asked.

"She said she'd read about the charming small town and the low cost of living. But you tell me. Have you ever heard of anyone giving up the Park Avenue life to live in small-town Ohio just because they read about the lower cost of living?"

Janice sang out, "'Darling, I love you, but give me Park Avenue.'"

They all laughed, and LuAnn said, "Welcome to Hooterville!"

Tess shook her head. Something wasn't adding up. "What do you think she's doing here then, if not house shopping?"

"I wish I knew."

Again, the women's eyes met. LuAnn reached into her purse and pulled out her notebook. "I'm adding that to the list of her suspicious behavior," she said.

Tess tapped the notebook. "Let's look over your whole list again."

"Someone needs to fill me in," Brad said, looking at the page of suspects. LuAnn gave him a quick overview of the mystery they were trying to solve, and just as she finished, the waitress arrived and set the pizza down in front of them. When they each had a slice on their plates, LuAnn looked down at her list.

"First we have Fiona. We know she's not an antiques expert but don't know what she's really doing here. She seems especially interested in the Underground Railroad tunnel, which would make sense if she's connected to the Twain treasure somehow. And she'd written a list of authors, including Mark Twain, on the notepad in her room."

"Which seems like a pretty amazing coincidence, considering Twain is right in the middle of this whole thing." Janice was using a knife and fork to cut her pizza into bite-size pieces.

"It does indeed." Tess hoisted her pizza and took a bite. "Though I have no idea how the other authors on that list are relevant, except for Harriet Beecher Stowe, who we know was his neighbor. And she wrote *Uncle Tom's Cabin*, which was a great boost for the abolitionist movement."

"Thoreau was also an ardent abolitionist," said LuAnn. "So I can understand why he's on the list. But I don't understand the others. Nathanial Hawthorne was well-known for his proslavery views. The other two, Melville and Irving, weren't involved in the politics of the issue at all, though I believe Washington Irving made it clear he thought slavery was evil. And people are still arguing about whether Herman Melville approved of slavery or not." She shrugged. "So there really is no rhyme or reason to who's included on the list—at least not that I can come up with."

Tess wasn't sure where to go from there. She had a feeling Fiona was tied up in this somehow, but couldn't see a clear connection.

"Who else is on your list?" Brad asked.

"Well, there's Helen," LuAnn said. "Is this whole house-hunting thing a ruse? An excuse to be here while she collects her money from the treasure?"

"Or is she waiting for the money she gets from the treasure to help her buy a house?" Tess asked.

"Fifty thousand dollars isn't chump change, but it's not enough to buy a house in this area," Janice said.

Brad pointed his fork at her. "You're right, but it would be a sizable down payment."

Tess considered this. "We'll keep her on the list," she said. "What about the newlyweds?"

"I haven't gotten much out of them," LuAnn said, and Tess and Janice agreed. "She seems to like thrift shops and antique malls, and he's not so into them, but other than that, I don't know a lot."

"They're here because they couldn't afford a more lavish honeymoon," Tess said.

Brad frowned. "Could they be here hoping to get the money to fund a more expensive honeymoon?"

"It's possible." LuAnn took a bite of her pizza, and the cheese stretched out in front of her. She laughed and set the slice down and wiped her fingers on a napkin.

"The only other guest who was around when the note was slipped under the door is Isaiah," Janice said. "But he went home this morning, so I don't see how it could be him."

"Plus, his alibi checked out. There really was a pet food convention in town," LuAnn said after she swallowed her bite.

"And it ended today, which was when he left," Janice added.

Tess thought about Isaiah. All of her interactions with him had seemed perfectly pleasant. She had no reason to believe he was anything other than what he said he was. But there was one thing that seemed, well, a tiny bit strange, if she was being honest.

"The only thing that felt a bit off was that he paid in cash."

"He did?" Janice's eyes widened.

"Which isn't necessarily a sign of anything," Tess said. "It could mean he'd just gone to the bank recently. Maybe he doesn't use credit cards for whatever reason. But so few people pay in cash, especially business travelers. I don't know. It's probably nothing."

"It's not nothing. Let's keep him on the list. But he still seems like the least likely suspect to me," LuAnn said.

"So it has to be one of those four possibilities," Tess said. "Since we know it's not one of us. But we have no way of knowing which one."

"Have you considered the other possibility?" Brad asked.

They all turned to him, waiting for him to go on.

"That Moses is making this whole thing up?"

"Why in the world would he do that?" LuAnn beat Tess to the question.

"I don't know. I'm just pointing out the possibility, since you're listing people who could be behind this whole thing."

Tess considered it for a moment. The first letter had been mailed to his home, Moses claimed, but he had no proof of who was actually sending it. The second had been slipped under his door, and no one else saw it happen. Someone had retrieved the note from behind the painting, but no one had seen who it was.

"It's possible," she said.

"But I can't see what benefit he would get out of it." Janice looked at LuAnn for her reaction.

"Unless there's a way he's trying to get the money from us somehow," LuAnn said.

Tess laughed. "There's no way he can get that much money from us."

"No, there isn't," Janice agreed. "*We* all know that. But perhaps *he* doesn't know that."

They considered this for a moment, and then, reluctantly, LuAnn added Moses's name to their list.

"There are still a few clues we're waiting on," Tess told Brad. "I have a friend trying to trace the phone number the text with the letter came from."

"And I'm working on piecing the shredded strips of paper together," Janice said. She explained to Brad what she was talking about. "When we see who threw out the bills, that may be a clue."

Tess didn't know what else to say. They needed answers now, more than ever.

Chapter Thirteen

It was nearing midmorning on Wednesday, when Janice came downstairs. Tess had been up for hours and had already eaten breakfast—an omelet and some of Winnie's freshly baked pumpkin nut bread—and checked in two new guests, sisters in their sixties who were spending a few days on a girls' trip. One would occupy Moonlight and Snowflakes, and the other, Woodbine and Roses on the third floor. Their shared sense of humor was evident as they remarked on every detail of the inn. But as soon as Janice came down the steps, Tess could see that she'd found something. Her face was pale and there were dark circles under her eyes, but there was a smile on her face. She held some papers—well, mostly tape, actually—in her hand.

"Where's LuAnn?" Janice asked.

"I'll go get her." Tess could see at once what Janice had. They were the strips of paper they'd found in the dumpster yesterday. Somehow she'd pieced a few of them back together. "Did you stay up all night?"

"Just about." Janice went to get coffee and then settled into one of the overstuffed chairs at the far corner of the parlor, where they'd be able to talk without the guests in the café seeing or hearing them. A minute later, they were all sitting with the papers spread out on the coffee table in front of them.

"I can't believe you really pieced these back together." LuAnn picked up the top paper, which was a phone bill. The strips of paper, less than half an inch wide each, were laminated together with clear tape.

"It was like piecing a quilt in some ways," Janice said.

"Except instead of beautiful fabrics, you were trying to match tiny, indecipherable writing," Tess said. It really was a feat, and she was grateful Janice had the patience for such painstaking work.

"But I'm afraid it doesn't really get us anywhere," Janice said.

Tess sighed and looked down at the papers. "Who in the world is Chloe Summers?" Each of the four bills on the table had been sent to a Chloe Summers at an address in Los Angeles.

"I've heard that name before," LuAnn said. "But for the life of me, I can't remember where."

"It sounds familiar to me too." Tess frowned. "But I don't have a clue why." She picked up an electric bill and shook her head. "None of our guests is named Chloe Summers, and none are from Los Angeles."

"At least, not that we know of," Janice said.

Tess saw what she was getting at. "You never did find a vintage shop in Chicago owned by Fiona, did you?" she asked.

"Nope." Janice shook her head.

LuAnn sat back and crossed her arms over her chest. "And you know what? Now that I think about it..." She let her voice drift off for a moment.

"What?" Janice asked.

"This may be nothing," LuAnn said.

Tess tapped the table. "But it may be something. So spill it."

"I was chatting with Fiona when she checked in. I was thinking she came from Chicago, so I asked about traffic getting out of the city. She laughed and said it was nothing compared to the 405 at rush hour."

"The 405?" Janice asked.

"It's a highway in Southern California," LuAnn said. "One that's famously always clogged with traffic."

They both looked at her.

"I spent a summer in Southern California." She shrugged. "You guys know I like to travel."

"So you think Fiona might really be from LA?" Janice asked.

"I think it's possible," LuAnn said. "It's the kind of comment that only someone very familiar with the freeways in Los Angeles would make."

Tess agreed. Add to that the fact that they already had Fiona on their radar because she'd lied about her job and because of the list of authors they'd found in her room.

"So how do we find out if Fiona is really Chloe Summers?" Tess asked.

"We do some research," Janice said at the same time LuAnn said, "We confront her."

Tess laughed. "How about this. We do some research on her, and then we confront her."

"That sounds like a good plan." Janice stood. "I'll see what I can find out about her after I get some breakfast." She stretched her arms over her head and let out a yawn.

"And maybe a nap," Tess offered.

"And maybe a nap." Janice smiled. "What are your plans for the day?"

"I was hoping to make some progress in the Mark Twain biography," LuAnn said. "To see if there are any clues that point to what he might have given Prudence and Jason, or any mention of time spent with the Underground Railroad, or anything like that."

"That sounds like a good plan," Tess said. She'd had an idea of what she wanted to do today, but it was nowhere near as pleasant as sitting in a cozy chair and reading a biography. "I was thinking I might dig through some old court records."

They both turned to her. LuAnn narrowed her eyes. Janice just looked confused.

She'd told them about the newspaper articles she'd uncovered yesterday. Now she explained that she wanted to find out what had happened to Peter Alexander, the thief who had been arrested for the robberies.

"If he went to jail in Washington County, there has to be a record of it," she said.

"But... I don't mean to be rude, but so what?" LuAnn said. "Even if he did go to jail here, how is that going to help you learn anything about where the Twain treasure ended up?"

"I'm not sure yet," Tess said. "I guess I'm hoping I'll know who to ask after I find out more."

It did sound like a wild-goose chase, now that she thought about it. But she wanted to know what had happened to the items Alexander had stolen, and this seemed to be a decent place to start.

"If only there was someone on the police force who knew the history of this," LuAnn said, shaking her head.

Tess agreed. "I wish for that too, but I'm afraid that person would be more than a hundred years old at this point. I don't think it's likely we'll learn anything that way. So I guess I'll start here and see if it gets us anywhere."

They heard footsteps on the stairs, and Janice hurriedly gathered up the papers. They didn't want any of the guests to see them and know what they'd been up to. Tess was relieved to see that it was just Sharon coming down the steps, a sleeping Sadie against her chest.

"I'm sorry to interrupt," she said. "I was hoping I could get something to eat." She brushed her finger lightly across the baby's downy head. "This little one fell asleep on me earlier, and I totally missed breakfast."

"What would you like?" Tess popped up and headed toward the café. "Breakfast is officially over, but we can certainly get something for you." Moses had taken Jack out earlier to explore the historic train cars on display in Harmar Village, leaving the exhausted mother and baby to sleep. "How about a muffin?"

"Anything you have is fine," Sharon said. "I'm so hungry I would eat anything."

"Please, sit." LuAnn steered her toward a chair while Tess went into the kitchen to get a leftover muffin. Winnie was already at work on a potato leek soup for lunch.

"Get a container of yogurt for her while you're at it," Winnie said after Tess explained her mission. "You're always hungry when you're nursing."

Tess took her advice and grabbed a container of yogurt as well as a muffin and carried them out to Sharon, who was resting on the couch, patting Sadie's back gently. Janice had vanished upstairs, and she could hear LuAnn clomping down the stairs that led to the basement. Laundry, no doubt. The never-ending laundry. Apparently the book would have to wait.

"Bless you," Sharon said, taking the muffin. Tess set the yogurt on the coffee table.

"Of course. Is there anything else I can get you?"

"I'm okay." Sharon smiled and took a bite of the muffin.

"Are you enjoying your stay?" As soon as the words were out of her mouth, Tess felt like an idiot. "I mean, considering."

Sharon laughed. "Yes, aside from the extortion, we're enjoying it here very much."

"I guess that was a silly question."

"No." Sharon took another bite and shook her head. "You all run a beautiful inn, and the service here is wonderful. You've really thought through every detail. Under different circumstances, this would be a dream vacation."

"Yes. Well, I hope you'll come back sometime under different circumstances." Tess hovered, unsure whether she should sit or let this weary mom have a few minutes of peace.

"I hope so too." Sharon adjusted her position on the couch, stretching her legs out in front of her. She gestured for Tess to sit. "But if we have to go through this anywhere, I'm grateful to be here."

Tess lowered herself onto the couch. Truthfully, she did have a few questions she wanted to ask Sharon.

"Have you heard about this Twain treasure before?" she asked.

Sharon pinched off a piece of the muffin and nodded as she put it into her mouth. She chewed, and then said, "Moses has mentioned it a few times over the years. And of course, it's a story that's been passed down in his family. His dad made references to it a few times, and at Christmas a few years back his grandmother told me all about it."

"What did she tell you?"

"Well, she wasn't a Willard when it was stolen," Sharon said. "She married into the family, but her family was very friendly with the Willards, and she was dating Moses—I don't know; I guess this was Moses the Third?" She shrugged. "Anyway, she remembered the robbery. It was shocking, of course. The first in a string of robberies that rocked the town, as she described it. It was a big deal, I guess."

"Did she tell you anything about…" Tess tried to figure out how to phrase this. "About what was in the safe?"

"You mean what the treasure was?"

Tess nodded.

"She didn't know."

"Oh."

"She did tell me that, based on the whispered conversations she'd overheard over the years, she thought there was more than sentimental value attached to the object that was stolen."

"You mean..."

"I mean that whatever it is, it is quite valuable." Sadie stirred, and Sharon patted her little back gently. "I guess that's why Moses is willing to consider paying what seems to be an exorbitant fee to get it back." She hesitated, then continued. "Well, that and the fact that he'd feel like he avenged his family somehow."

"The newspaper article I read about the theft indicated that the object was of sentimental value."

"I'm sure it was. But I don't think that was the whole story." Sharon laughed. "After all, they don't call it the Twain keepsake."

"I guess that's true."

Sadie stirred again, and Sharon kissed the top of her head.

"She's precious," Tess said. "Where did the name Sadie come from?"

Sharon polished off the last of the muffin and brushed the crumbs off her fingers. "I just liked it. Everyone always wants names to have *meaning* these days. Like, it has to be a family name or have some special meaning in Sanskrit or Gaelic or whatever. But I don't know. It's so much pressure. Our parents just picked names they liked. So I did the same."

Tess smiled. It was kind of refreshing. "And I noticed that you didn't name your son Moses."

Sharon raised her eyebrow. "No, I figured that name had run its course in that family."

Tess laughed out loud. "Not a fan?"

"I don't mind the name. I just don't think it's the *only* name. There are plenty of good names out there. Plenty of good biblical names, even, if that's what floats your boat."

"Did Moses fight for Moses the Sixth?"

She lifted her chin, just a bit. "My husband knows how to pick his battles."

Tess laughed again. Sharon had spunk. She liked that.

"You settled on John."

"A perfectly noble biblical name."

"It is indeed."

Sharon smiled and pushed herself up slowly. "If it's all right, I'll take this yogurt upstairs. I'd love to try to get a shower while she's asleep, if I can do it without waking her up."

"Good luck." Tess wanted to volunteer to watch the baby so Sharon could take a shower but wasn't sure if that would be crossing a line. Would Sharon be grateful or find it worrisome to leave someone she barely knew in charge of her daughter? She wasn't sure what to do, and in the end, she let Sharon go upstairs without saying anything. Tess stood up and bit her lip. Janice, timid as she was, was so good about being bold when it came to helping people.

Oh well. Next time. Tess thought for a moment about their guests. Helen had left with Brad to do some more house shopping, and the newlyweds had gone out not long ago, after a leisurely breakfast at the café. And Fiona was...actually, she wasn't sure where Fiona was. Had she gone out this morning? She had no idea. Well, she'd ask Janice and LuAnn to keep an eye on her.

But for now, Tess had to get going. She had a date at the county commissioner's office. Well, not a date so much as an appointment to look at dusty old records. She'd determined online that vital records, including court and prison records, were kept there. If she wanted to find out what had happened to Peter Alexander, it seemed like the right place to start.

She checked in with LuAnn and Janice, and a few minutes later, she was walking along the sidewalks next to the cobblestone streets. Tess loved how most of the town was within walking distance of the inn—it saved gas and wear and tear on her car, meant she didn't have to worry about parking, and gave her some exercise to boot. It only took a few minutes to reach the stone-and-stucco building on Putnam Street. It was tucked up right next to the county courthouse, and the triangular pediments over the windows gave the building a Federal-style look. Late-season celosia, mums, and Michaelmas-daisies bloomed in planters outside.

She made her way inside and asked at the front desk for help finding prison records. The woman at the desk directed her to a room in the basement where such records were kept. "Ask at the desk downstairs. Shawn will help you find what you need."

Tess made her way down the basement stairs and found herself at the end of a long hallway. There was a desk at the far end, but no one was there. She started down the hallway, her footsteps echoing on the tile floor, and as she approached the desk, a man appeared from one of the rooms, carrying a box crammed full of papers. He was probably in his late forties, with brown hair that could use a trim, and a rumpled button-down shirt and khakis.

"Hello!" He gave a cheerful smile. "Are you here to look through records?"

He seemed a little too excited about the prospect.

"I'm trying to find the answer to a strange question," Tess said.

"My favorite kind." He set the box down and smiled again. "I'm Shawn," he said, and held out his hand.

"Tess." She accepted his handshake. "I'm trying to find out what happened to a man who was arrested for robbery in 1928."

"Oh boy." He rubbed his hands together. "You do like a challenge. Do you know his name?"

"Peter Alexander."

Shawn led her to a room lined on all sides with file cabinets, and started digging through yellowed manila folders and delicate old papers. He seemed to know the files very well, and Tess was grateful for his enthusiasm, because from the looks of this room she'd never figure out where to even start. Shawn hummed to himself as he looked through papers, shoving drawers closed and opening others.

"Here we go."

He set a folder on the table and opened the cover. He took a minute to skim through a few pages.

"In here is a record of court proceedings that indicate Peter Alexander was sentenced to twenty-five years at the Washington County Jail," he said. "The old one, not the new one across the river," he added. Tess nodded as if this made sense, though she wasn't familiar with either jail.

"What happened to him after that?" she asked.

"Let's find out." The guy was so excited about all this that Tess might find it unsettling if it weren't so thoroughly useful. It only took him a few minutes of searching on a computer at his desk—explaining that some records had been digitized but it was spotty at best—to find out that Peter had died in prison in 1942.

"Can you find out what happened to the things he stole?" she asked.

"Well now. That might be more of a challenge. It will take some digging. Do you have some time?"

"Sure."

He turned to his computer and started mumbling to himself as his fingers flew over the keys. Then he vanished into one of the rooms that branched off the hallway.

Tess sat down in a molded plastic chair near the desk to wait. She checked her phone to see if Kent had called her back, but there was no message from him. She did have a voice mail from Lizzie, though. She held the phone to her ear to listen.

"Hi Mom, I'm sorry for the last-minute request but I was hoping you'd be able to take the kids for a few hours tonight. I've got a bunch of parents coming in for parent-teacher conferences, but Michael is sick, and it would be a huge help if you could watch them for a couple of hours. Can you let me know?"

Tess set the phone in her lap and thought about how to respond. Of course she'd take the kids—she loved to see her grandkids. She was glad for any excuse to take care of them.

Never the Twain Shall Meet

But something about it still rankled. Lizzie was glad to turn to good ol' Mom when she needed help, but couldn't fit her in for Thanksgiving? It didn't seem right.

Tess knew Lizzie was overwhelmed, with the triplets and her job. She knew most days her daughter was barely hanging on. Lizzie had called on Tess many times, and Tess had always been glad to help. Lizzie would have no idea that her mom was feeling put upon.

But shouldn't she know? Shouldn't she realize how it looked to ask for help now, after saying Tess wasn't welcome for the holiday?

Tess hated how childish she felt thinking these thoughts, but she couldn't deny the feelings.

She turned her phone over and over in her hands, thinking through how to respond. But there was only one way she could respond, of course. She pressed Call.

"Hi, Lizzie," Tess said.

"Hi, Mom. You got my message?"

"I did. And of course I'd be happy to watch the kids." Tess knew Lizzie was expecting her to come over to their place. But why couldn't she bring the triplets to her for once? "Would you be able to bring them here?"

Lizzie hesitated, just for a second, and then said, "Of course. Is five thirty okay?"

"That's great," Tess said.

"Thanks, Mom. I really appreciate it."

Tess hung up, unsure what to think. She was excited to see the kids—being with them always brought so much joy and energy to her life. But something about the interaction with Lizzie still gnawed at her. Did Lizzie take advantage of her? She'd never really thought about it. Lizzie was her daughter. Of course Tess helped her out whenever she could. But this time... Tess shook her head. Something about this was different.

"I found it!" Shawn came back into the hallway, holding a folder aloft. "I found the records from Peter Alexander's file."

"What does it say?"

"Everything the police recovered was returned to the owners."

Tess thought this through. "So if something *wasn't* recovered, that means..."

"That it couldn't have been returned to the owner."

Tess let out a sigh.

"I'm sorry. Doesn't sound like that was what you wanted to hear."

"No, not exactly."

"Hmm." He thought for a minute. "I guess you could always see if this guy had any family. Ask them if they know anything."

"You think I should find a great-grandchild and randomly ask if they know what happened to something his or her ancestor stole almost a century ago?"

He shrugged. "You never know what you might find. Stranger things have happened."

She thought it would be pretty strange indeed if she found anything this way, but still... "So how would I find his descendants, if I wanted to? Assuming he had any, of course."

"Oh that's easy. We've got birth, marriage, and death records here. Property records too. Do you want to look yourself, or would you rather I take a look?"

Tess had had her fill of digging through hard-to-read historical records in the past few days. "You can go for it."

A smile crossed his face, and Tess wanted to laugh. She guessed she should be grateful for people who enjoyed this kind of research. He started by typing something into the computer, and then he went into one of the rooms down the hallway again. Tess wondered what he was doing. She'd thought some of these kinds of records were private, but apparently not if you came in and asked the right person. A few minutes later, Shawn returned with a piece of lined notebook paper in his hand.

"Here it is." He handed the paper to her. There was an address underneath the name. "There's a great-grandson named Jordan Hayes." He smiled even brighter, if such a thing was possible. "And get this. He lives here in Marietta."

"Really?" Tess still thought it was unlikely there was any chance an ancestor would know about the missing Twain treasure, but she took the paper anyway.

"I hope this helps," he said.

"It's great. Thank you so much." Tess folded the paper, put it into her purse, and stood to go. "I appreciate your help."

"Come back if you have any more 'strange' questions." He gave her a jaunty wave, and she turned and headed back up the stairs.

Tess started to walk back home, but before she'd even made it to the first corner, she stopped. She recognized the name of the street where Jordan lived. It was only a few blocks from here. What could it hurt, really, to swing by and see if he knew anything? Chances were he wouldn't know a thing, and that would be that. Tess realized she was hesitating because she was afraid of looking foolish. He would probably think she was nuts—if he was home at all. But what if he did know something and she completely missed it because she was too afraid to ask?

She pulled her phone out of her purse and used an app to find the house. She'd just go by there and see if anyone was home. She turned right onto Fifth Street. The address Shawn had given her was on Tupper Road, a narrow one-way street paved with brick that bordered Mound Cemetery, the historic graveyard that was built around an ancient burial mound. Tess walked down the street, which was lined with mature trees and older homes, and wondered what it would be like to live across from a cemetery. At least the neighbors would be quiet.

She found the address Shawn had given her. It was a two-story wood-frame home with a large front porch and a balcony that wrapped around the front of the second floor. It was cozy and charming, with a small lawn and a stone path that went around the side of the house. There was a driveway with a minivan parked in it.

Tess took a deep breath and knocked on the door. She heard footsteps inside, and a moment later the door was pulled open. A woman stood there with a toddler on her hip. She had a bob haircut frosted a shade of blonde, and she wore a loose shirt over yoga pants.

"Hi," Tess said. At once she recognized the familiar chaos of a home with small children. There were toys strewn across the floor, the smell of burnt toast in the air. The television was on in the living room, and a little boy sat in front of it, transfixed, watching a show about talking trains. "My name is Tessa Wallace, and I own Wayfarers Inn with a couple of my friends."

"Oh yeah." The woman's face brightened. "With Mrs. Eastman, right?"

Tess nodded.

"I remember her. She taught Home Ec at the high school." She shifted the toddler to her other hip. "I wonder if she'd remember me. Of course, I wasn't a blonde then. And my maiden name was Sharp. Jodi Sharp."

"It's nice to meet you, Jodi." Tess felt a tiny bit of her nervousness drain away. "Did you take any of her classes?"

"I did." Jodi laughed and gestured at the mess behind her. "Though you couldn't tell it from this mess."

Tess laughed along with her. "I have what is probably a strange question."

Jodi didn't get excited the way Shawn had at this pronouncement. Instead, she tilted her head.

"I'm trying to track down something that was stolen almost a century ago"—as the words came out, she realized how crazy it sounded— "and it turns out Jordan Hayes is a descendant of the thief. Do you know Jordan Hayes?"

Jodi nodded. "That's my husband. You're talking about his great-grandfather or whatever who robbed all those places in town?"

Tess nodded. "You've heard about it?"

"Oh yeah. Jordan is proud to have such a scoundrel in his lineage. He thinks it's funny."

Tess wasn't sure what was funny about it, but then, she didn't claim to understand young people these days.

"Jordan is a church deacon and works for a nonprofit," Jodi explained. "He's about as far from a scoundrel as you can get. So, I don't know, I guess he likes the irony."

That made a little more sense. "The thing is, some of the things his great-grandfather stole were never recovered, and I'm trying to find out what happened to one of them. I know it's a total long shot, but I thought I would at least ask in case anyone here knew where any of the items might be."

"I have no idea, I'm afraid," Jodi said. The toddler in her arms squirmed, and she set him down. He scampered off and joined his brother on the couch. "And I'm pretty sure Jordan doesn't either. That was, like, ages ago."

Tess nodded. It was what she'd expected, after all. She started to thank the woman, but then Jodi snapped her fingers.

"Oh! Wait... There's a bunch of boxes of junk that were in Jordan's grandma's attic."

"What?"

"Jordan's grandma had this big old house on Fourth Street," she said. Tess nodded. There were some beautiful large old homes in that part of town. "When she passed away last year, the whole family pitched in to clean out the place to sell it, and she had so much junk up in that attic. I don't even know what all was there, but most of it had been there for decades, at least. I think a lot of it had been there since before her time. She'd inherited the house from her parents, so there was generations worth of stuff up there."

Tess felt her pulse speed up. Was it possible the treasure had been tucked away in an attic all these years? "What happened to it?"

"Oh, we got rid of just about all of it." She shrugged. "The family members kept a few things, but most of it was either donated or just tossed in the trash."

Tossed in the trash? Tess didn't even want to think about the possibility that the treasure had been thrown away. Then again, she reasoned, someone claimed to have it now, which meant there was a good chance it had survived somehow.

"What was it? The thing you're looking for, I mean?"

"I don't know." Tess felt silly admitting it. "All I know is that it had a connection to Mark Twain. But I don't know if that was obvious or what the object was."

Jodi scratched her ankle with her toes. "Well, I'm afraid I'm not sure how to help you then. All I can say is that we threw out a bunch of stuff and donated the rest of it to Goodwill. I'm not sure where it would have ended up after that, unfortunately."

"Thank you," Tess said, unsure what else to say. She turned to go. Even if the Twain treasure had been among the things they'd donated, there would be no way to track it down now, especially since Tess didn't know what she was looking for. Still, something Jodi said stuck in her mind.

The family had donated things to Goodwill. And Lindy Marlowe had said that she loved scouring thrift stores. She'd said she liked to look for vintage jewelry, but was it possible that she'd come across something else as she was hunting?

She thought back through her interactions with the newlywed couple. Lindy had said this was her first time in Marietta, hadn't she? Tess wasn't sure if she had said that or if Tess had just assumed it. But even if she had said that, she could have been lying. And the couple had indicated that they didn't have much money. Had Brad guessed what was going on here? Were Richard and Lindy hoping this honeymoon could turn into a way to fund the honeymoon they really wanted?

Tess headed home, turning all these thoughts around in her mind, trying to figure out how to make sense of them. When she was still a few blocks away from the inn, her phone rang. She dug it out.

"Hello?" She held the cold plastic to her ear.

"Tess? This is Kent Gavin. I looked into tracing the number that text came from."

"Did you find out anything?"

Kent chuckled. "You're not going to believe this."

Chapter Fourteen

But before I tell you the part you won't believe, let me tell you this. It's a burner," he said.

Tess pressed the phone against her ear. She couldn't have heard that right. "A what?"

"A burner phone. A throwaway phone."

"Who would throw away a phone?"

He wasn't making any sense.

"You can buy them in any drugstore. They're just prepaid phones. Untraceable, unfortunately, since there's no contract and no registration. You just buy the phone, use it, and throw it away when you're done."

"That seems wasteful."

"Usually people who buy burner phones aren't worried about their environmental footprint."

Tess thought about this for a moment. "You're saying people buy these phones when they don't want to be traced."

"Exactly."

Tess felt her hopes deflate. "So there's no way to know who sent that text after all."

"Hang on. Don't give up yet. I have good news too."

"Hit me."

Kent laughed. "Well, I can't tell you who had the phone. I can't trace that part of it. But we can still track the phone's general location."

"Really?"

"The phone still had to access a cell tower to send the message. And we can use that to find a general location."

"What did you find?"

"This is the part you won't believe. It seems the text was sent from your inn, or very near to it, anyway."

Tess felt her heart rate speed up. "So it had to be someone at the inn who sent the text."

"Or someone very close to it. The technology isn't perfect, to be honest, so I'd give the location tracking a margin of error of half a mile or so."

A half mile? That could be anywhere. Still, it confirmed what they'd suspected, that it was most likely someone at the inn. Someone who'd been at the inn yesterday afternoon.

"Thank you for your help," she said.

"Of course. Any time." He paused, and then said softly, "Take care of yourself, Tess."

"I will." Tess felt a rush of affection for him. Jeffrey had loved and trusted Kent, and he had been so helpful in the days after Jeffrey's death. She appreciated that he was looking out for her even now.

She made it back to the inn and once again realized she'd missed lunch. She ate a quick sandwich and filled Janice and LuAnn in on what she'd discovered.

Never the Twain Shall Meet

"So you're saying it could have been Lindy and Richard after all," LuAnn said. "She could have found the treasure at a thrift store, recognized what it was, and called Moses here to sell it to him."

"Fifty thousand dollars would be quite a nest egg to get your marriage started." Janice had a cup of hot tea in front of her, and she wrapped her fingers around the warmth.

"Let's try to talk to them when they come back," LuAnn said. "In the meantime, I'll head back to my Twain biography." She tapped the thick book in front of her. "I'm learning all kinds of interesting facts."

"Anything useful for solving the mystery?"

"Not yet," LuAnn said. "The book hasn't yet mentioned a mysterious treasure he sent to some Quaker abolitionists." She gave them a wry grin. "But I did learn that he lost a lot of the money he made publishing books by investing in a new printing technology that never took off."

"Well, that's sad," Tess said.

"He kept writing, trying to have another success like *Huckleberry Finn* to make up for it. He even published a few more books about Huck Finn and Tom Sawyer—*Tom Sawyer Abroad* and *Tom Sawyer, Detective*—but they never quite worked."

"It would be hard to repeat a masterpiece like that," Tess said.

"He tried," LuAnn said. "He started a couple of other sequels. The one he got the furthest on was called *Huck Finn and Tom Sawyer Among the Indians*. In this one, Tom and Huck go west."

Tess thought for a moment. "Do you think there's any chance—"

"No," LuAnn said, shaking her head. "Sadly not. I hoped that too. But we know what happened to that book. He abandoned it about fifteen thousand words in, but it's been published, along with a number of his other unfinished stories. So the treasure can't be a lost sequel, sadly."

Janice shook her head. "That's a shame. How cool would that be?"

"To uncover a lost manuscript by one of the greatest writers in our country's history?" LuAnn spread her arms. "It would be amazing. But not possible, I'm afraid. We'll have to keep thinking."

Janice let out a noise that was somewhere between a moan and a sigh.

"But get this. He was actually a very generous man," LuAnn continued. "Did you know that he paid for several African-American men to go to college, and a couple of women as well?"

"Wow." Tess hadn't known that. "He did more than oppose slavery, then. He tried to actually help the people affected by it."

"Exactly." LuAnn nodded. She picked up the book and headed upstairs, and Tess went downstairs to do some laundry.

When she got to the basement, she stared, as she often did, at the locked door that led to the tunnel that ran out to the river. It was hard to imagine that escaped slaves had made their way through that tunnel to freedom. Tess couldn't imagine the courage it must have taken, both for the people who risked everything on the hope of finding freedom, and for the people who risked it all to help them find it. Tess hoped she'd have had the kind of courage Prudence had displayed. She prayed she would, if the need ever arose.

Tess sighed. It would take a different kind of courage to face that pile of laundry.

She turned and started toward the laundry room but then stopped. She'd heard something. Footsteps, down at the end of the hallway. "Hello?"

And then, the creak of a door on its hinges.

"Hello?" Tess called again. LuAnn had gone upstairs to read, and Janice had said she was going to clean the guest rooms. Had one of them come down here instead? "LuAnn? Janice?"

Tess started down the hallway, lined on both sides with small, spare rooms that had once served as quarters for the workers at the inn—and for the runaway slaves they were trying to pass off as workers. "Winnie, is that you?"

What would Winnie be doing down here? Tess made her way down the hallway toward the door to the garden. The noise had been down at the end of the hallway, she thought, but she stopped and peeked inside each room anyway. "Hello?"

Had she imagined it? Maybe she hadn't really heard the footsteps. And a breeze could have blown the door. Tess knew it was silly, though. How could there be a breeze down here? She got to the last door and pushed against it. "Hello?"

The door swung open, and Fiona blinked at her, as if surprised to find her here. She had her phone in her hand, and before she shoved it into her pocket, Tess saw that it was set to the camera app.

"Oh! Hello!" Fiona's voice was unnaturally cheerful. "These rooms are so amazing. Is this where the runaway slaves were hidden?"

Tess didn't even know how to respond. What was Fiona doing down here?

"I'm afraid guests aren't supposed to be down here, which I believe we already told you," she said.

"Oh, I'm sorry, I know you'd said that. But I am so fascinated by the Underground Railroad, and I saw the door to the basement open, and I—" Fiona shrugged. "I'm sorry, my curiosity got the better of me. I hope you'll forgive me. I love history, what with the antiques and all."

Tess nodded, but in her mind she wasn't agreeing. She was confused, angry. The door to the basement hadn't been open. They never left it open. It had been closed when Tess came home, and it hadn't been opened until she opened it to come down here. So why was Fiona lying? And what was she really doing in the basement? Tess gestured for her to come out of the small room, and Fiona complied, her smile never faltering.

"Where did you say you're from again?" Tess closed the door to the small room as they stepped back into the hallway.

"Chicago," Fiona said, her voice still just a tad too bright. Today she was wearing black skinny jeans and ankle boots, along with a chunky sweater and glasses. Had she worn glasses before? Tess didn't remember seeing them.

"Is that where you're from originally?" Fiona's voice didn't have an accent that belied a Midwestern upbringing.

"Oh no," Fiona said. "I was born in Pasadena, and lived there until I went away to college in Chicago."

Tess tried to keep her voice neutral. "Where did you go to school?"

Fiona paused for just a second too long. "The University of Chicago," she said.

I bet you did, Tess thought. But she had no way to prove the young woman was lying. "What was your major?" Tess led her back down the hallway toward the stairs.

Fiona looked at her. "History."

Tess wasn't sure whether to believe her or not. It made sense, if she was so interested in the Underground Railroad.

"What about literature?" Tess asked. "Do you have any interest in that?" She couldn't come out and say why she was asking, she realized, without revealing that she'd been snooping in Fiona's room. But she could still ask.

"Sure. I like books. I never really studied literature, but I do like to read."

They'd reached the top of the steps, and they stepped into the café area.

"Thanks so much for letting me take a look!" Fiona said, and bounded up the stairs before Tess could point out that she *hadn't* let her.

Tess mulled over the incident a few minutes later as she loaded laundry into the washing machine and took a load of towels out of the dryer. What had Fiona been doing down here?

She spent the next few hours tidying up and looking over bills and upcoming reservations, then spent a few minutes chatting with the sisters who'd checked in that morning. They were visiting from Pittsburgh, and had heard about the inn from a couple at their church who had come to stay a few weeks back. Tess was thrilled to hear that word-of-mouth advertising had brought them here.

"It's wonderful to come to a place where history is so alive," said the older one, who'd introduced herself as Maryann.

"I don't really care where we go," her sister Grace said. "A few days away from cooking and cleaning? Yes, please."

The women laughed and went out to do some shopping, and a little while later, Moses came in from an excursion with his family and said he had some news. Once Tess had gathered Janice and LuAnn, and Sharon and the kids had vanished upstairs, he showed them a text he'd received that afternoon.

Meet me on the Harmar Bridge tomorrow at nine pm. Come alone. Bring a cashier's check. I will have the treasure.

"Wow." LuAnn's eyes were wide. "So, are you going to do it?"

"I guess," Moses said.

"We'll go with you," Tess said.

Janice looked at her with raised eyebrows. "It says to come alone."

"Well, he can't very well go *alone*, can he?" Tess said. "That's just silly." She turned to Moses. "And you can hardly put your wife and family in danger."

"But he can put *us* in danger?" Janice said quietly.

"Tess is right," LuAnn said. "We'll go to keep an eye on things. Make sure you're safe."

"Um..." Moses looked from Tess to LuAnn and Janice and back again. "Thanks, but..."

Tess saw he was doubting the wisdom of inviting three sixty-something women along to be his bodyguards.

"We'll stay in the shadows. Just be there to keep an eye on things, in case anything goes wrong," she assured him.

"No one will suspect us of being involved," LuAnn added. "If we're seen, we'll just say we're out for a stroll."

Janice rolled her eyes. "Out for a stroll at nine o'clock on a Thursday night in November?"

LuAnn ignored her and plowed on. "That's the great thing about being this age. Everyone underestimates you, so you can get away with anything."

Moses laughed at that. "Well, I don't know about that, but I suppose if you three ladies were somehow near the bridge on your own, it wouldn't be my fault."

"Exactly." Tess put her hand on his arm. "We'll be there. Only, you know, not *right* there. And of course you don't know—for sure—that we'll be there. We might just decide not to come."

"Exactly." LuAnn said.

Janice still looked uncertain. "What about bringing someone else along too? Maybe it's time to bring in the police. Chief Mayfield would be willing to help, I'm sure."

Moses hesitated. "Maybe." After a pause, he said, "I would just hate for the person with the treasure to see the police and be scared away."

"Maybe Brad, then," Janice suggested.

The others seemed to consider it, but no one answered.

"Oh, Tess, tell him what you found out about who was sending the texts," LuAnn said, changing the subject smoothly.

Moses's face brightened, full of fresh hope. Naked hope, which made Tess hate the news she had to deliver all the more.

"I'm afraid it's a big fat nothing," she said. "All I can tell you is that there's no way to find out who is sending the texts."

Disappointment washed over his face. "Burner phone?"

Tess nodded. "I'm sorry. But we still have some ideas about who it could be."

"Well, I guess I'll find out tomorrow night, in any case," he said.

It was true, he would find out on the bridge who was behind all this. But figuring it out ahead of time would help them prepare, and maybe even help Moses retrieve the treasure without paying the exorbitant ransom.

Moses headed upstairs just as Helen came into the inn, followed by Brad.

"Hi there," Janice said as they stepped inside. "How did it go today?"

"Oh, we saw some wonderful homes," Helen said. "Brad took me to see a brand-new house, and it was so nice to imagine just moving right in and having everything be new."

Tess looked at Brad. Hadn't he said she'd really wanted something with historic charm?

"Imagine, being the first one to use the kitchen and the bathroom," Helen went on. "No one else's dirt anywhere. It sounds divine."

"It does," Tess agreed. It did sound appealing. But you couldn't have all that and historic character too. What did Helen really want? It was becoming clearer every day that she didn't have a clue what she was looking for.

"If you'll excuse me," Helen said, "I'd like to change before dinner."

"Of course." Janice stepped back so Helen could get to the stairs.

As soon as she'd reached the second floor and was out of earshot, LuAnn said, "New construction?"

"She specifically asked to see something brand-new," Brad said. "So what could I do?"

"Do you think she'd really buy something brand-new?"

Brad sighed. "I'm less and less sure she really wants to buy anything, to be honest."

"Do you think the real estate hunt is just an excuse for something else?" Janice asked.

"Maybe, but for what? I really have no idea," he said.

Tess looked up the stairs to make sure they weren't being overheard. "Were you able to learn anything more about her today?"

"I found out she's recently separated from her husband. I get the sense he was some powerful businessman and she was used to him making all the decisions," Brad said. "So this is really the first decision she's gotten to make on her own in a long time. And I think that the sudden freedom is sort of paralyzing."

Tess was surprised, not at the information, but at Brad's insightful interpretation of the situation.

"That does make sense," Janice said, and LuAnn nodded.

"Oh, and there's one other thing," Brad said. They all looked at him. "You've been summoned."

Janice's eyes grew wide, while LuAnn laughed out loud.

"The aunts," Tess said. Brad's aunts were Thelma and Irene Bickerton, fixtures of Marietta's high society. They lived in a huge historic home, and though it was recently revealed that Brad and his brother, Grant, were actually the rightful heirs of the old Bickerton home and family fortune, Thelma and Irene had spent a lifetime having their orders obeyed, and they weren't about to give it up now.

"Exactly," Brad said.

Tess thought about her schedule. "When do they want us to come?"

"This evening, if possible," Brad said. "I told them you can't just drop everything and run out to see them, but you know how they are."

Tess glanced at the clock on the wall behind the check-in desk. There was only about an hour before Lizzie was supposed to bring the kids by.

"If we go right now, there should be time," she said.

"Perfect." LuAnn started up the stairs. "Let me grab my coat."

Janice followed her. "I'll be right back down."

A few minutes later, they pulled into the driveway of the Bickerton home. They made their way up the path across the wide, sloping lawn. The Bickerton house was a three-story stone structure with leaded glass windows and a wraparound porch. Turrets rose up on the corners, and a carriage house sat next to it, topped with a copper weather vane.

Tess rang the doorbell, and they were shown in by a quiet woman in black. Tess knew that Thelma and Irene liked to have someone help them with cooking and cleaning for several hours a week, but they never seemed to keep the same woman for long, since Winnie left and came to work at the inn. The woman led them to the library, where Thelma and Irene sat side by side on a velvet settee.

"Come in." Thelma's invitation sounded more like a command. She gestured toward the wing chairs upholstered in a rich brocade and the loveseat, covered in the same fabric. With the wallpaper in a burgundy, turquoise, and gold paisley and the walls of bookcases lined with leather spines, the whole tableau was a bit disorienting. Janice and LuAnn settled into the chairs while Tess sat down on the love seat. It was stiff as plywood.

"So," Irene said. At eighty-eight, she was the younger of the two sisters, and though she wasn't even five feet tall, she could intimidate even the hardiest soul. Tess looked around, taking in the heavy marble fireplace and the statues, framed photos, and vintage musical instruments that decorated every surface. This room must be a challenge to dust.

"I bet you're wondering why we've asked you here," Thelma said. She fingered the gold locket that hung over her gauzy pink blouse.

Asked was hardly the right word, Tess thought. But then she looked from one aunt to the other and wondered... Why *had* they been called here? Could these bastions of Marietta society possibly know something about the treasure? Tess quickly did some math in her head. Thelma was ninety-four. That would make her...well, she would have been a child when the treasure had been stolen. It was unlikely she would remember much, if anything, about the robbery itself. But was it possible she knew something about the treasure?

"We were curious," LuAnn admitted.

"Does it have anything to do with Mark Twain?" Tess asked.

The wrinkled brows and evident confusion on their faces was all the answer she needed.

"What in the world does Mark Twain have to do with anything?" Thelma said.

LuAnn laughed, and Janice shook her head.

"Never mind. Nothing." Tess gestured for her to go on. "You were saying?"

"We just wondered why you're having our nephew take that awful Chloe Summers all over town," Thelma said.

"What?" Now the three of them were the confused ones.

"Chloe Summers is...Helen?" Janice said tentatively.

"I have no idea what she's calling herself," Irene said. "All I know is that it's her." She reached for a magazine that was on the console table behind the settee.

"See?" She flipped open the pages and held it up. Tess saw right away that she had opened to an article about Conner Summers, an investor who had recently been arrested for running a Ponzi scheme. He'd collected money from investors impressed by his high rate of return, but it had recently come to light that he actually had no investments at all—he'd just been collecting money from new investors to pay off the people who had already entrusted their money to him. It was a classic house of cards that had collapsed in a spectacular and very public way because many of his investors had been high-profile athletes and Hollywood celebrities.

"She's related to Conner Summers?" LuAnn's eyes were wide.

"She's right here," Irene said, turning the page. And there she was—it was Helen, next to Conner Summers, outside the courthouse in downtown Manhattan. She tapped the page. "After her husband cheated hundreds of people out of millions of dollars, she has the nerve to complain to the magazine about having to sell her home. *Homes*," she corrected. "Look at this. They had homes in Los Angeles, Aspen, Manhattan, Miami, and Provence. Don't you feel bad for her?"

"Oh my." Janice shook her head. "No wonder she's using an alias."

"But wait." Tess shook her head. "I read about this. Wasn't it proven that she had no knowledge of what her husband was doing? None of it was her fault, right?"

"Maybe, but she sure didn't mind living the high life while it lasted," Thelma said, sniffing.

Tess had to force herself to suppress a smile, thinking of Thelma and Irene here in this house they didn't own, living off a fortune that actually belonged to Brad and Grant.

"Well, it's no wonder she's moving as far away from any of those places as she can get," LuAnn said.

"And why she has no idea what she wants." Now Brad's assessment that this was the first time Helen, aka Chloe, had been on her own, having to fend for herself, made sense. In a very real way, he was right.

"We didn't know who she was," Tess insisted.

"We'd figured out that there was someone named Chloe Summers staying at the inn," Janice clarified. "We just didn't put it together that it was Helen."

Irene's face showed shocked dismay, and Thelma huffed. "Really. This is national news," she said. "And that...that woman, she thinks she's going to just waltz in here and take up residence in our town without anyone knowing who she is? Does she think we're all a bunch of naive provincials?"

"Well, now that we know who she is, we'll make sure to take care of it," LuAnn said.

Thelma huffed again, and Irene adjusted her seat on the couch.

That was it, then. They were dismissed.

"We really must get going," Tess said, pushing herself up. "I'm babysitting the triplets tonight."

Neither woman acknowledged the comment as the others rose as well. The nameless maid, who had somehow materialized at just the right moment, escorted them to the door.

"Well, that was enlightening," LuAnn said in the car as she buckled herself in.

"That's one word for it." Janice shook her head. "I can't believe we missed it."

"I knew the name Chloe Summers was familiar," Tess said. "I just couldn't place it."

As they backed out of the driveway, Janice looked at LuAnn in the rearview mirror. "You said we were going to take care of it, LuAnn. What did you mean?"

LuAnn laughed. "What I meant was that we were going to extend the same grace to Helen—I mean Chloe—that we would to any guest who passes through our doors. We'll tell her that her secret is safe with us and let her know we will help her any way we can."

"Oh good." Janice nodded. "I was thinking the same thing. From everything I read, she really didn't know about what her husband was doing."

"I agree," Tess said. "And she seems to be a victim as much as anyone else. She's lost everything, and is just trying to start over."

"Good. So we're all in agreement about that." LuAnn braked for a red light at the corner of Putnam Street.

"The real question is, how desperate is she to start over?" Janice asked.

"You mean..." Tess was pretty sure what Janice was thinking.

"I mean, just because we know who she really is, it doesn't mean she couldn't be the one with the Twain treasure," Janice said. "In fact, now that we know she used to have a lot of money, it seems even more possible she's behind all of this. She could have gotten the treasure any number of places."

LuAnn started moving forward as the light turned green. "But it's not like she could have bought it at an auction at Christie's. Not if it's stolen."

"Oh, LuAnn," Tess said. "If you have money, you can acquire anything. You know rich people buy things on the black market all the time."

"I guess the upshot is, we know who she is, but can't eliminate her as a suspect," Janice said.

"I think you're right." Tess sighed.

A minute later, they pulled into the driveway, with Lizzie's minivan following just behind. Tess hopped out as Lizzie opened the sliding side door. Liam, who'd recently learned to unbuckle his car seat, hopped out and ran toward her.

"Mimi!"

Tess's heart melted at the sight of him. His chubby little legs pumped as he ran across the grass. A moment later, Henry came running up to her, and Harper followed just a few paces behind.

"Come here." Tess ducked down and wrapped all three of them in a hug and as they all tried to get close, they nearly pushed her over. "Oh, it's so good to see you little lovies," she said.

"I'm not little," Harper insisted. "I'm three."

"Of course you're not little." Tess straightened up and pushed herself back to standing. "Are you ready to come inside?"

"Yeah!" Liam did some kind of a karate kick, and Henry, less coordinated than his brother, attempted it as well and knocked himself right over.

Janice and LuAnn had already gone inside, and as the kids ran in ahead of Tess, Lizzie yelled, "Be quiet! Don't run!" She hoisted a tote bag that Tess knew from experience was filled with sippy cups, snack bags, blankets, and some spare Pull-Ups for Henry, who still had accidents sometimes.

"It's okay," Tess said. "It's early enough that hopefully no one is trying to sleep yet."

"Thank you for doing this, Mom."

"Of course." She smiled, though something inside her ached as she said it. "It turns out I'd take any opportunity to see my grandkids."

Did that come out a bit more barbed than she'd intended it to? Lizzie didn't seem to notice, so Tess decided she was probably overreacting. "How's Michael?"

"He's got a fever," Lizzie said. "And you know how men get when they're sick."

Tess laughed. Jeffrey had always seemed to be on his deathbed whenever he got a head cold.

"It'll be good for him to be able to rest," she said. She gestured Lizzie inside. "I just hope the kids don't get it."

"Ugh." Lizzie shook her head. "Me too. Get down," she called to Liam, who was somehow already jumping on the couch. He had a scrape on his nose—from his tumble off the slide, she remembered. "Henry, don't you dare touch that piano."

Tess marveled, as she often did, at how Lizzie managed to always have an eye on all three kids at once. But her attention was always scattered. With the three of them plus her teaching, it was no wonder she needed to focus all her energy on Michael's parents.

But then, why not have Tess help her? Wouldn't it make more sense for her to have an extra set of hands around to help deal with the kids?

"I won't be late," Lizzie said. "I'll do my best to get the parents out of there as quick as possible tonight."

"Don't worry about it," Tess said.

"Well, I need to get them to bed." Lizzie looked around, taking a few deep breaths and taking in the cornucopias on the mantel and the apples and cinnamon smell in the air. "It sure looks and smells like Thanksgiving in here," she said. She set the tote bag on the coffee table.

Tess smiled. "We tried."

Lizzie nodded. "So you have a lot of reservations for your dinner?"

"Yes, it looks like it's going to be a full house," Tess said. "LuAnn has planned the menu and Winnie will do the shopping for us. Our guests aren't coming until midafternoon, and we're going to do as much cooking as we can ahead of time, so we should be in pretty good shape."

What was that look on Lizzie's face?

"That's good. I'm sure you'll have a lot of fun getting ready for that." She almost looked a bit wistful. Was it possible...

"We're going to be crazy with Michael's family coming in," she continued. "Did I tell you that his younger brother is now bringing his new girlfriend?"

"Wow. It sounds like you'll have a full house too."

"Our other grandma always gives us chocolate when we want it," Henry said.

"And she always brings us presents," Harper added.

Tess laughed. Subtlety wasn't one of her grandchildren's strong suits. "And I'm sure she's looking forward to seeing you."

"Yeah." Lizzie gave Tess another look that she couldn't make out, but then caught sight of the clock behind the check-in desk.

"I'm sorry, Mom, I've got to run."

"Go. Have fun. We'll be here."

"Thank you."

Lizzie dashed out, and Tess turned to the kids. "Should we head upstairs?"

The kids fought over who got to push the button on the elevator, but soon she had them all crouched over bowls of macaroni and cheese, and after that, they all sat around the television in the common area and watched a Minions movie. Henry and Harper each snuggled under one arm, while Liam sprawled on the floor in front of them. Tess loved snuggling with her three precious grandchildren. It was a perfect evening.

Then she thought back to Lizzie's face as she'd mentioned Thanksgiving.

Make that *almost* a perfect evening.

Chapter Fifteen

The two sisters from Pittsburgh were the first down to breakfast the next morning.

"Oh, this smells so wonderful," Grace said, inhaling deeply.

"Do you have those amazing lemon ricotta pancakes again? Those were so delicious," Maryann said.

Tess had recently returned from a long walk along the river, and now that she thought about it, pancakes sounded really good to her as well.

"I don't know, but let's find out," she said. The women took a seat at one of the café tables. Taylor came over and took their order, and if Tess wasn't mistaken, they were definitely flirting with him. The poor boy. Tess gave him an encouraging smile and asked for an order of pancakes for herself.

As Tess ate, she skimmed the headlines in the local paper, and then LuAnn came out of the kitchen carrying her own plate of pancakes.

"Mind if I join you?"

"Please." Tess folded the newspaper and put it aside, clearing a space for LuAnn. "How does Winnie make these so light and fluffy? I've never had pancakes quite this delicious before."

"She whips the egg whites," LuAnn said. "And doesn't over-mix the batter. She swears that's the secret, but I don't know. It doesn't seem like enough somehow. And you know how she likes to hold back at least one key element when she shares a recipe. Job security, she calls it."

"Well, I'm just glad she works for us and not our competitors," Janice said. She cut a piece and swirled it around in the Vermont 100 percent maple syrup. Tess hadn't splurged on that very often when it was just her and Jeffrey, but Winnie insisted on the real thing, and she had to admit it was light years better than the stuff made from corn syrup. "How are you this morning?"

LuAnn shrugged. "I didn't sleep very well, to be honest."

"Me neither," Tess admitted. She'd lain awake for a good while thinking about Lizzie, and about the kids, and about Michael and his family, trying not to be hurt all over again as she thought through their conversation about Thanksgiving. Finally, after praying for God to change her heart and allow her to be happy for and support Lizzie no matter what, she was able to drift off. "What were you thinking about?"

"The showdown on the bridge tonight."

Tess laughed, though it wasn't at all funny. "Surely it won't be a showdown."

"Who knows what will happen? I was talking with Moses last night, and he was thinking he might bring a real cashier's check and a fake one, and see how it goes. I don't know if that's the best plan or not, but I do think it could go badly. I'm thinking it actually might be a good idea to get the police involved."

"I kind of agree. I guess we'll need to work on convincing Moses." Tess took a sip of her coffee.

"I guess how it goes down depends on who's the one with the treasure," LuAnn said. "My money is on Helen."

"You mean Chloe?" Tess used her fork to cut off another bite of pancake.

"Whoever she is, I think she had the opportunity to get a hold of the treasure, what with her connections among high society in New York," LuAnn said. "I was doing some research last night and read that a few years ago she bought a Picasso at an auction for a record-setting price."

"Be that as it may, we all agreed that what her husband did wasn't her fault," Tess said.

"Sure, it wasn't her fault, and sure, we need to show her grace and love. But that doesn't mean she wouldn't try to get whatever she could for the treasure."

Tess thought about this. "But if she has access to the expensive auction houses, why wouldn't she take the treasure there and try to get as much as she possibly could for it?"

"Because she can't admit to having anything valuable," LuAnn explained. "The Feds seized all her possessions, remember? She was able to keep some clothes, and that's about it. Everything else was taken away by the government to be sold off. If she was somehow able to sneak the treasure out, under the table is the only way she'd be able to sell it."

It made a certain amount of sense, Tess thought as she considered it.

"And she has an obvious motive, because she needs a chunk of change to start her new life here in Ohio."

"True, although any of our suspects could use the cash," Tess said. "What about the newlyweds?"

"Well, sure. Richard and Lindy could use the money, I guess."

"They want to take a real honeymoon. Not to mention the cost of tuition these days. And I'm sure they'd love to get something in savings for a house or baby. And don't forget there's a good chance the treasure ended up at a thrift store. We know that Lindy spends a lot of time looking through thrift stores."

LuAnn took a bite and chewed as she thought for a moment. "I guess there's one other point in their favor," she said.

"What's that?"

"Moses is a big man," LuAnn explained. "It's kind of hard to imagine either Helen or Fiona agreeing to meet him by themselves on the bridge in the middle of the night. If it's Richard *and* Lindy, that makes a bit more sense."

"True enough," Tess agreed. She ran another piece of the pancake through her syrup. "But my money is still on Fiona."

"It *was* strange how you found her poking around the basement," LuAnn said.

"And how we found Twain on the list of authors in her room. And how she's obviously not an antiques dealer but she won't tell us what she's doing here."

Tess took the last bite of her pancake and sat back. "I guess we just keep trying to figure it out," she said. "At least until we see who shows up at the bridge tonight."

LuAnn shrugged. "I guess so."

Just then, Fiona came down the stairs, and a moment later, Janice followed. Tess and LuAnn looked at each other. The timing there was strange, Tess thought. It was almost as if Janice had been waiting for her.

"Fiona," Janice called, stepping onto the lobby floor just behind their guest.

Fiona turned, and her eyes widened when she saw Janice directly behind her. "Yes?" She quickly put a smile on her face, but in that split second, they'd all seen that she was not thrilled to find Janice following her.

"I have a question for you," Janice said. Once again, Tess glanced at LuAnn, whose eyes were wide. She'd heard it too, then. That was Janice's pastor's wife voice. She was up to something.

"What's that?" Fiona was wearing some kind of tight athletic pants and sneakers with a leather jacket over a white T-shirt. She had sunglasses perched on her head, a backpack slung over one shoulder, and a phone in a sparkly case in her hand.

"I noticed yesterday that your car was a rental," Janice said. Fiona didn't answer, so she continued. "There's a little sticker on the windshield. It was rented from the same company where a friend from my church works."

"Oh?" Fiona raised her eyebrows.

"I wondered why you would have rented a car if you drove here from Chicago," Janice said.

"Oh, I don't have my own car," Fiona said. "A lot of people who live in the city don't."

"That's true," Janice said. "But if you were coming here to look at antiques for your store, why wouldn't you have rented a bigger vehicle? One that could haul everything back?"

Tess couldn't believe it. Janice was interrogating Fiona. She had ambushed her and was now demanding answers. Tess was confused, but totally thrilled.

"I'm having it all shipped," Fiona said.

By the look on LuAnn's face, she couldn't believe it either.

"The thing is, I couldn't find your shop," Janice said. "I researched all the vintage stores in Wicker Park, and none of them had ever heard of you."

"It's new." Fiona's answer sounded ridiculous, and they all knew it.

"Well, but then I asked my friend at the car rental agency," Janice said. "Annette has been a dear friend for years. We both sang in the church choir back when my husband was the pastor. She has the most beautiful alto voice you've ever heard."

Fiona stood there, waiting.

Janice was grilling Fiona, and she was nailing it. Where had their timid friend found the courage?

"Anyway, I asked Annette for a favor, and she was happy to look something up for me. She was able to pull up the driver's license used to rent the car. And it turns out you're not from Chicago after all. You live in California."

"Who is this person, and what has she done with Janice?" LuAnn whispered.

"I don't know, but I like her," Tess said under her breath.

"I am from California," Fiona said. "I told Tess that. I grew up in Pasadena."

"But the license was renewed just last year, and to an address in Los Angeles."

Several emotions flashed across Fiona's face, and then she finally shook her head.

"Okay. Fine. So what?" she finally said. "I'm from California, not Chicago. So what's the big deal?"

"The big deal," Janice said, "is that we're trying to figure out why you've lied to us."

Fiona didn't move or say anything. Then she shifted her weight from one foot to the other. And then, slowly, something in her face began to change. The fight had gone out of her, or something. Finally, she took a deep breath, let out a sigh, and said, "Okay. You want to know the truth?"

Janice nodded. "Preferably the whole truth."

Fiona nodded and breathed out again.

"I'm a location scout."

"A what, now?"

"For a film company. I'm working on a film about the Underground Railroad, and the producer is trying to decide whether to shoot the film in Marietta or some place in Indiana. I think your inn would be perfect, what with the tunnel and the historic downtown and everything. So I've been looking for different places to film scenes and taking pictures to try to build a case for this place."

"You're...you're what?" Janice's brow wrinkled. "Wait a minute...how do we know you're telling the truth this time?"

Fiona reached into her phone case and pulled out a business card. "Here's my card," she said. "It has the phone number and email address of the company I work for. You can call them and ask them about me, if you want."

Janice took the card from her. "Are you saying your company might want to make a film here? In the inn?"

"Maybe." She shrugged. "Ideally. But it's not my call. The producer is the one who decides in the end."

"How..." Janice shook her head. "Do you pay to rent the spaces where you film?"

"Yep. That's why I don't tell people what I'm really up to. They either ask about how much they'd make or they ask to be in the movie."

"I don't want to be in a movie," Janice said, shuddering. Tess stifled a smile, as she saw LuAnn already starting to bounce in her seat. LuAnn would take a role in the film, no doubt about it. "But we just started the inn. We sure could use the exposure and would love to rent it out."

"Well, like I said, it's not my call. But I do think this town would be perfect. So I'm going to let the producer know that this is my vote."

"Wow." Janice looked at the card in her hand again. "That's great."

"Yep." Fiona reached into her backpack and pulled out her wallet. "The reason I was coming downstairs was to check out. I've got all the information and pictures I need. Would it be okay if I leave a day early? My company will still pay for the extra night."

"Oh." Janice seemed confused. "So you're...you're going to the airport?"

"Yep. Changed my flight this morning and everything. And look—" She swiped her phone a couple of times and then held it so Janice could see the screen. "It's a flight to Los Angeles."

"Well...I'm sorry you'll be leaving early," Janice said. "It would've been nice to get to know the real Fiona." She smiled, and Tess knew she didn't want the words to sound resentful.

"Yeah, well. I'm sorry I wasn't honest about what I was really doing here."

"I understand," Janice said. She took Fiona's credit card and went behind the check-in desk to process her paperwork. After a few minutes she said, "When are you leaving?"

"As soon as I pack up my things." Fiona took the card and tucked the wallet back into her bag. "Thanks so much."

"What about the list of authors?" Janice asked.

Fiona's brow wrinkled.

Oh dear. Janice probably shouldn't have brought that up. Tess went into a minor panic attack. How was Janice going to explain how she knew Fiona had written a list of author names in her room without revealing that they'd been snooping?

"There was a list of authors in your room." Janice went on confidently, either not realizing or just ignoring the difficulty of the situation. "It had names like Hawthorne, Thoreau, Twain, and Stowe on it."

"Oh, that." Fiona shrugged. If she thought the question was weird, she didn't show it. "I was looking at your bookshelves down here and was impressed by the collection. But of course for our shoot, we would need to make sure only authors who published before the Civil War were on the shelves. You'd be surprised how many people catch things like that. So I spent some time on the internet coming up with a list of authors whose books could be shown on the bookshelves of the inn if we do a shoot here."

Tess's grasp on the history of American literature was shaky at best, but judging by LuAnn's face, Fiona must be right about the list of authors. LuAnn shook her head.

"How did I miss that?" she muttered under her breath.

"Well, thanks for a great stay," Fiona said. She turned and headed back up the stairs.

As soon as she was out of earshot, LuAnn called, "Janice! Get over here."

Janice grinned and came to join them.

"What in the world?" LuAnn stared at her. "Who *are* you?"

"What do you mean?" A light pink flush spread up Janice's cheeks, but she was still smiling.

"That was awesome," Tess said. "You totally confronted her and demanded answers, and she crumbled."

"I just—"

"I didn't think you had it in you!" LuAnn said.

"Goodness gracious goat, you two are acting like something extraordinary really happened here." Janice smoothed down her tan sweater.

"I've just never seen you do that," Tess said.

"Well, I just got so mad," Janice said. "I was up for hours last night, thinking about it. I couldn't get over the fact that she was lying to us. I kept thinking, she knows she's lying, *we* know she's lying, but we just act like it's okay and none of us have had the guts to call her on it."

"So you planned a sneak attack," LuAnn said.

"I did." Janice nodded sheepishly. "I just... I don't know what happened. I just had to get her to admit the truth."

"Well I'm very glad you did," Tess said. "Because it worked."

"I can't believe I didn't pick up on the fact that those were all pre-Civil War authors," LuAnn said. "I feel like a... Well, let's just say I hope my students never find out."

"You're retired." Tess laughed. "Give yourself a break."

"It's just that...honestly, Mark Twain threw me off. *The Adventures of Huckleberry Finn* and *The Adventures of Tom Sawyer* were both set before the Civil War, but they weren't published until the 1870s and 1880s. Really, only his very earliest stories were published during the War." LuAnn shook her head. "But still. I should have picked up on it."

Tess didn't see how LuAnn could have figured out what that list of authors was truly about. "It doesn't matter at all. At least now we know who she really is and what she was doing here," she said.

"Well, if what she said is all true, then she's not the one with the Twain treasure," LuAnn said.

"I guess not." Tess hadn't expected to feel so disappointed at that realization. They could cross another suspect off their list.

But that meant there was only a handful left.

And they were running out of time to figure it out.

Chapter Sixteen

Tess was going a little stir-crazy by midmorning. She was a bundle of nervous energy, and making her way through the never-ending chore list wasn't helping. Already she'd updated the inn's website, returned emails regarding event rentals, and blown through several loads of laundry. She'd even written real snail-mail letters thanking those who had made reservations for their Thanksgiving dinner and telling them how much she was looking forward to meeting them. Janice was cleaning the guest rooms within an inch of their lives, and LuAnn kept dropping things in the kitchen.

When Richard and Lindy came downstairs, Tess pounced. Janice had been so awesome at getting Fiona to tell the truth about what she was doing here. Tess was ready to try it too.

"Hello there!" she called out as they made their way down the last few stairs. "How are you this morning?"

"Just fine," Richard said.

"It's the last day of our vacation." Lindy stuck out her bottom lip.

They were due to check out tomorrow, Tess had already noted. The timing was just a tad bit too convenient, in her opinion.

"So what are you going to do on your last day in town?" she asked.

"Probably poke around some more junk stores," Richard said, deadpan. Lindy smacked him on the arm.

"We're going to see some lovely shops," she said. "And we have a reservation at the Buckley House tonight, so that will be our last big hurrah before we head back to real life."

"Have you found any treasures in the stores you've visited so far?" Tess asked. She hadn't intentionally used the word *treasure*, but it slipped out. She must have treasure on the brain.

"I found a few great pieces of costume jewelry that just need to be cleaned up," Lindy said.

"And a cake carrier. Don't forget that cake carrier." Richard was helping himself to the coffee. "Everyone needs one of those."

"You just watch. You'll be glad we have it someday." Lindy turned back to Tess. "It's a cool vintage one made out of tin, and it has this retro pattern all over it. It's awesome."

"You can never have too many cake carriers," Richard said.

Their dynamic was so funny, Tess thought. He loved her, that was clear, even with all of his sarcasm. But Tess forced herself to focus on her mission.

"What was the best thing you've ever found in a thrift store?" Tess tried to keep her voice level, as if she was just curious.

"Hmm." Lindy tilted her head.

"Surely it was the cake carrier," Richard said. Lindy dismissed his comment with a wave and kept thinking.

"One time I found these really cool old advertisements for Western Michigan, which is where I grew up. They showed the

Mackinac Bridge and people playing on the beach in these retro bathing suits."

"The 'beach.'" Richard rolled his eyes and made air quotes.

"Lake Michigan has real beaches," Lindy insisted. "You can't even see all the way across or anything." She turned back to Tess. "He grew up in Hawaii, so no other beach will ever measure up."

Tess could see that this was a familiar argument, and one she didn't intend to get in the middle of. "Have you *ever* found anything valuable at a thrift store?"

"I think we can all agree on the inestimable value of a properly carried cake." Richard was now sipping his coffee, watching his wife over the rim of the cup.

She ignored him.

"Not really," she said. "I mean, not in any real way. You mean like a priceless artifact buried among the junk?"

"Exactly."

"Not yet, I'm afraid." She sighed. "You read about these stories of people finding paintings by famous artists and things like that, but I've never found anything along those lines."

"But you'd better believe she's going to keep looking." Richard held out a coffee cup to Lindy, who took it and shook her head.

"You know you love poking through those stores as much as I do."

"I love whatever you love."

Lindy started toward the door, and he followed a few steps behind. "Save me," he mouthed dramatically at Tess he stepped outside.

Tess wanted to laugh, because as much as he pretended to hate being dragged around to thrift stores, she suspected he enjoyed it as much as his wife did. But she was also trying to decide whether to believe Lindy or not.

She wouldn't exactly confess, even if she had found the Twain treasure, would she? Now that she considered it, Tess thought it was really unlikely that Lindy would say anything at all about finding anything valuable, even if it were true. But something inside her believed Lindy. Maybe it was her earnest, open countenance. She came across as genuine. But, then again, maybe she was just a really good actress.

Tess wasn't any closer to knowing for sure whether they were involved than she had been a few moments ago. And unfortunately, there were very few moments left.

Chapter Seventeen

After lunch, the inn was quiet. Moses and Sharon had taken the kids out to burn off some energy before Jack's nap, and the other guests were also out. The three women of the Inn Crowd were trying to find ways to keep themselves occupied, but an almost palpable sense of urgency hung in the air. Janice was working on her quilt, and though Tess usually found the soft rhythmic hum of her sewing machine soothing, today it was irritating her. LuAnn was sitting on the couch in their sitting room, reading the Twain biography. Tess didn't know what to do, so she started straightening the small upstairs kitchen, even though it was already in perfect order.

The sounds of Tess's phone startled them all. She grabbed it and saw that it was Lizzie. She quickly walked out of the living room and into her own suite before she put the phone to her ear.

"Hi, Lizzie."

She was probably calling to say she'd realized she hadn't really said thank you for watching the kids last night.

"Hi, Mom." Tess could hear the low hum of talking in the background.

"Are you at work?"

"Yes. My students are in gym class, so I thought I'd give you a call."

"I'm glad you did." Tess didn't mind watching the kids, no matter what, but it was still nice when someone said they appreciated it. "What's up?"

Then again, Lizzie was so busy. Last night she'd been gathering three tired three-year-olds into the car after spending all night talking to her students' parents. No wonder she'd been in a rush to get home. It didn't really matter that Lizzie hadn't said—

"I wondered if I could borrow that big serving platter for Thanksgiving. The one that you always used for turkey when we were growing up?"

"Oh." Tess felt the air whoosh out of her lungs. Lizzie wasn't calling to apologize at all but to ask for something. "The Blue Danube one?" The serving platter didn't match the rest of her china, which was Wedgewood's Wild Strawberry pattern, and it had a few chips, but she had picked up the platter at a garage sale many years ago and had used it just about every holiday since.

"Yeah, the blue-and-white one. Are you going to be using it? And if not, could I?"

"I—" Truthfully, she hadn't really thought about what kind of dishes they'd be using for their Thanksgiving meal here at the inn. Did LuAnn own any china? Would they use china at all, or would they just stick to the everyday dinnerware? She had no idea.

But that wasn't really what had her flummoxed. Was Lizzie really hoping to borrow her platter to serve a meal Tess wasn't invited to? She didn't want to let herself get upset, but she felt her frustration rising.

"If you're using it, that's okay. I'll find something. It's just that... I don't know. I always associate it with Thanksgiving, so it would be really special to use it this year, you know?"

Tess didn't feel the tears well up until they spilled over. She took a deep breath, trying to steady herself.

"Yes, it is a very special platter," she said, trying to keep her voice as calm as possible. No sense in letting Lizzie know how much she'd upset her. "And I guess you can use it. It...it won't feel like Thanksgiving here without you anyway, so you might as well use it."

"Mom..." Lizzie sounded uncertain. "Are you—"

"I'm sure Michael's family will have a lovely time. You can pick up the platter anytime. Now I'm afraid I have to go."

Tess ended the call and flopped down onto her bed. The comforter rose up a bit and then settled. Tears streamed down her cheeks.

It was silly to rush off the phone like that. She knew she'd acted like a child. But how could Lizzie... Did she really not see...

Tess's phone rang again, and Lizzie's name flashed on the screen. Tess silenced it. Probably calling to ask about the gravy boat too.

Tess knew she was being unkind. But it sure felt like Lizzie was too. Didn't she see how much it hurt to not invite her own mother to Thanksgiving? To choose Michael's family over her?

Tess lay on her bed and cried for a while, letting herself mope. The Bible said the Lord was near to the brokenhearted, but sometimes it didn't really feel like it. Still, Tess prayed for peace, and for the grace to be kind and generous to her daughter, no matter what she was feeling.

Then, when she felt calmer, she got up off the bed and stood by the window for a moment. The river sparkled in the sunlight, and a few boats went up and down. The sun was shining, and it was a beautiful day. This was her new life, she thought. She got to live in this amazing place, with this amazing view. It was different, but it was good.

She turned away from the window and went into her bathroom to splash cold water on her face. She took a few deep breaths and decided she looked almost normal again. Her eyes were still a bit red, but that would fade. Then she steadied herself and went back out into the sitting room.

"Oh, Tess, what's wrong?" Janice was looking at her with a mixture of confusion and concern.

All righty, then. Apparently she'd been mistaken about looking almost normal.

"It's okay. It's just Lizzie."

"Is she okay? Is one of the kids hurt?"

"No, no. Nothing like that. No one's hurt. It's just about plans for Thanksgiving. It's..." Tess considered, and then she realized she didn't want to rehash it all now. "It's fine."

"But Tess—"

"You guys."

Both Tess and Janice turned toward LuAnn, who was still sitting on the couch. She had the biography of Mark Twin open, but she was looking at them, her eyes wide. "I think I found something."

"Found what?" Tess asked. Why was LuAnn looking at them like that, like she'd seen a ghost?

"I know who will be on that bridge tonight."

Chapter Eighteen

"What do you mean you know who'll be on the bridge?" Janice had stood and was walking toward the couch. Tess also moved closer to see what had made LuAnn so excited. "You found the answer in that book?"

"I think I did," LuAnn said. "Get this. You know Mark Twain is a pen name, right?"

"Right," Tess said. "His real name was Samuel Langhorne Clemens. We know that."

"I just can't believe I missed it," LuAnn said. She shook her head and laughed. "Even with the Moses connection right under our nose, we totally missed it."

"What Moses connection?" Janice asked.

"What did we miss?" Tess sat down in one of the wing chairs and gestured for her to spit it out.

LuAnn set the book in her lap. "Moses Willard writes his books under a pen name, right?"

"Right." Janice nodded.

"How did he pick his pen name?" LuAnn asked.

"I don't know." Tess shrugged.

But Janice knew. "He talked about that in one of the interviews I read online. He said Sherman is his mother's maiden name. And Matt was the name of the bully in his elementary school, the one who always picked on him for being a nerd. It was his way of showing he'd triumphed over the bully and made it *because* he was a nerd. He also hoped using the name would give him a chance to share the story with kids and encourage them to stand up to bullying."

"In other words, he picked a name that had meaning for him," LuAnn said.

"So is Mark Twain the name of a bully from the nineteenth century?" Janice wrinkled her brow.

"I thought it was some nautical reference?" Tess had heard that somewhere, many years back. Maybe in high school?

"It is that," LuAnn said. "It came from his time as a riverboat captain." She looked down at her book and read from it. "Listen to this. 'The riverboats had to travel in water that was at least two fathoms deep.'"

"How much is a fathom?" Janice asked. "I've always wondered that."

"I think it's about the same as a cubit," Tess joked. Despite the word *cubit* being used throughout the Old Testament, she'd never met anyone who actually knew how big a cubit was.

Janice threw a pillow at her.

"I don't know how deep a fathom is, but it doesn't really matter. Listen. 'The word *twain* is an ancient term for two.'"

"Like 'never the twain shall meet,'" Janice said.

"Exactly," LuAnn said. "So out on the river, when the water was deep enough for a boat to safely pass through, the riverboat men would yell, 'by the mark, twain,' which meant, 'according to the mark, or the line, the water is two fathoms deep and safe to pass through.'"

"I had no idea that's where his pen name came from," Tess said. "It's clever."

"It is clever," LuAnn said. "But it's not original."

"What do you mean?" Tess asked.

"Samuel Clemens was actually not the first writer to use that pen name," LuAnn continued.

"Wait. Really?" Janice sat down beside LuAnn on the couch.

"According to this book, there was another man, another riverboat captain, in fact, who used the name Mark Twain as his pseudonym first. This other Mark Twain published articles in a few newspapers, but he never published anything that gave him great notoriety. When he died, and would no longer be using the name, Clemens adopted it as his own."

"Huh," Tess said. "Can you do that? Use someone else's pen name?"

LuAnn shrugged. "I guess you can. It appears no one stopped him, in any case. But that's not the most interesting part. Get this."

They both looked at her. Tess realized she was holding her breath.

"The man who used the name Mark Twain first?" LuAnn was enjoying this, drawing it out.

"Yes?" Tess said.

"His name was Isaiah Sellers."

It took a moment for Tess to understand.

"W-wait, like our guest Isaiah Sellers?" Janice finally stammered.

"Like the man who checked in here using the name Isaiah Sellers," LuAnn answered. "I don't know what his real name is, but it can't be an accident that he used that name."

"You think he's the one with the Twain treasure," Tess repeated, trying to wrap her head around the idea.

"I think it *has* to be him. He's the one who will be meeting Moses on that bridge tonight," LuAnn said. "It only makes sense."

"Wait." Tess could see that LuAnn had made the jump from the name to assuming he was their man. But Tess wasn't there yet. "Maybe he just happens to have the same name." But even as the words came out of her mouth, she realized how silly they sounded.

"It would be an amazing coincidence," Janice said quietly.

"But..." Tess shook her head. She'd written him off as a suspect. How had she gotten it so wrong? "But he really did go to a pet food convention," she insisted. "That was why he was here, and he really went."

"We know there was a pet food convention in town," LuAnn said. "But do we know that he actually went to it? Isn't it possible he did exactly what you did and found out what conventions and meetings were happening in town, and picked one of them as an alibi?"

Tess had to admit there was some logic to it.

"But he went home on Tuesday," she protested.

"No, he checked out on Tuesday," LuAnn said. "We don't know where he went from here. But I bet he's still in the area somewhere."

"The communications went from notes to texts around the time he checked out," Janice pointed out. "And your man in the police chief's office said whoever was sending the texts was nearby."

"But..." Tess knew it was futile. The evidence that she'd misinterpreted everything was mounting. "But he showed me pictures of his kids." It sounded lame and she knew it. There was no law that extortionists couldn't have children.

"What did they look like?" Janice reached over and picked up her laptop, which was on the table. She flipped the lid up.

"The girl had blonde hair and blue eyes, and the boy had brown hair and brown eyes. Maddie and Collin, he said."

"What were Maddie and Collin wearing?" Janice's fingers flew over the keys.

Tess tried to remember. "Easter clothes was my guess. Dressy and pastel."

A moment later, Janice turned the computer around and a gallery of pictures of children was on the screen.

"What is this?" LuAnn asked.

"Stock photos." She tilted the screen so they could see better. "Do any of these look familiar?"

Tess nodded. There it was, in the second row. "That one." She pointed to the picture of the girl and the boy she'd seen on Isaiah's phone. He'd picked their photo out of a gallery and downloaded it.

"So they're not really his children," she said quietly.

"Well, technically there is an infinitesimal possibility that they really are his children, and they were the models for this shot. But it's much more likely that he did his homework and wanted to have a picture ready in case anyone asked him about his family. When you search for 'smiling children' at the stock art site, it's one of the first photos to come up."

"And didn't you say he paid cash for his room?" LuAnn asked.

"Oh my." Tess let her head sink into her hands. Paying cash would mean he didn't have to use a credit card, which would show his real name. "That's right. He did." How had she not seen that as a clue? "He just seemed so...nice. So unlikely."

"But why would he check in using a name that ties him directly to Mark Twain?" Janice asked.

LuAnn shrugged. "Maybe he thought we weren't going to make the connection. Or maybe he thought that even if we did, it didn't matter."

"Wow." Tess closed her eyes and leaned back in her chair, letting it all sink in. "So you think he's the one who's going to show up on that bridge tonight with the treasure."

"I believe he is responsible for this whole thing," LuAnn said. "The one who sent the note to Moses, and the one who claims to have the treasure. But does he really have it? That I don't know. We don't know if it even exists anymore, or what it even is. Or was."

"I suppose the real question is, who is he really?" Janice said. "I guess that's the first step in figuring this whole thing out."

Tess glanced down at her watch. "And we only have about eight hours to find out."

Chapter Nineteen

They spent the next few hours doing everything they could to uncover the real identity of the man they knew as Isaiah Sellers, but they kept hitting dead ends. The address he'd given them when he'd checked in turned out not to exist, and the phone number he'd used when he registered proved to belong to a teenage girl in Missouri, who let them know that she did not appreciate them calling her.

Janice called the Goodwill donation station where Jodi Hayes said they'd donated the stuff from her husband's grandmother's house, and was told that the goods they collected there were gathered into a central facility to be sorted and then distributed to stores all over the area. There wasn't any way to trace where a particular item had ended up.

LuAnn was busy trying to figure out what exactly the treasure was, hoping that would give them some insight into what they were looking for. "It had to be small enough to fit in a safe," she said.

"And it was not just valuable for sentimental reasons," Tess added. "Sharon told me she got the impression from Moses's family that it also had high monetary value."

"Don't forget what Prudence said about it," Tess said. "Whatever it was, its very existence put her and Jason at risk."

"But what in the world would it be?" LuAnn's frustration was evident in her voice.

No one had any idea. But they didn't give up.

Tess tried to use everything she knew about the man who went as Isaiah Sellers to figure out who he really was. But without a real name, any contact information, or any idea where he was really from, there was nothing to go on.

She finally threw her hands up in frustration. "Well, ladies, if there's one thing we've learned through all of this, it's how important it is that we see valid ID from our guests when they check in."

"I suppose we'll have to start 'carding' people," Janice said sadly. "But who knew it could happen three times in one week?"

Tess groaned. "What are we missing? How can we find out who this guy really is?"

"Let's think about this for a minute," LuAnn said. "He stayed here at the inn for two nights, right?"

Tess nodded.

"He went out during the day. Do we have any idea where he really went? Assuming attending the pet food convention was a ruse?"

Janice shook her head. "No, but we know that even after he checked out, he stayed in town, and he was not far from the inn when he sent that text. Your friend the police chief couldn't say exactly how far away, right, Tess?"

"Right." Tess nodded. "He couldn't give us an exact number, but he suggested a half-mile radius."

"So let's assume he stayed in town after he checked out," LuAnn said.

"Or maybe he lives in town."

"But none of us have ever seen him before," Janice said.

"There are plenty of people in town we've never met," Tess said. "I know you've lived here for a long time, but surely you don't know everyone."

Janice yielded. "True. Well, in any case, if the text came from within a half mile of the inn, it can't be that hard to find out if anyone has seen him in the last day or two."

"If we had a picture of him, we could show it to the businesspeople around here," LuAnn said.

Tess thought for a minute. Hadn't someone... Fiona took pictures of the inn, but Tess didn't remember seeing her and Isaiah Sellers in the same room together. But—Tess closed her eyes and tried to visualize this—hadn't he been in the café when Sharon was taking selfies of herself and the kids the other day?

"We should ask Sharon."

"Sharon?"

Tess explained her thinking, and they reasoned that they needed to tell Moses what they'd discovered anyway, so a few minutes later, the whole Willard family was in their sitting room.

"So it was Isaiah?" Moses asked, shaking his head. Jack was pressing his face against the glass of the window that overlooked the river, and Sharon had set Sadie down on a blanket on the floor.

"It was the man who called himself Isaiah," Janice clarified. They explained how they'd figured that out, and then Tess told them her idea.

"Remember Monday morning at breakfast, when you were taking pictures?" she asked Sharon.

"Vaguely." Sharon grimaced. "I don't remember a whole lot these days, if I'm honest."

"A newborn will do that to you," Janice said.

"Here." Sharon pulled out her phone and started scrolling through pictures. "Here are the pictures from that morning. And here's where Jack started taking pictures."

She held out her phone, and LuAnn, who was the closest, took it and began to flip from one picture to the next. Janice and Tess peeked over her shoulder. The first few were nice shots of Sharon and the two kids, and after that, Jack had taken probably a dozen pictures of the room at various angles.

"There he is," LuAnn said. Tess saw that she was right. Isaiah was in a couple of the shots, his back turned to the camera, but in one, Jack had caught him walking out of the café, his iPad under his arm.

"That's him," Janice said quietly.

"Could you forward that to us?" Tess asked.

LuAnn handed the phone back to Sharon. She typed in their numbers and shared the photo with them.

"All right then, ladies," LuAnn said. "I say we take this photo and go out and talk to as many people within a half-mile radius as we can. Should we divide and conquer?"

A few minutes later, they had mapped out sections of the area around the inn to visit. After asking Winnie to watch the front desk, they headed out. It helped that the river was directly in front of the inn, so they didn't have to worry about hitting up any businesses on that side.

Tess's first stop was the Sassy Seamstress.

"Hi, Tess," Wendy Wilson, the store's owner and Brad's niece, called out as Tess walked in the door. Tess appreciated the colorful displays of fabrics Wendy had carefully arranged, but as Tess was a total disaster at crafts, her appreciation never led to a sale. "What can I help you with?"

"I'm wondering if you've seen this man," Tess said, holding out her phone.

"Hmm." Wendy tilted her head. "He doesn't look familiar. Who is he?"

"That's what we're trying to find out," Tess said.

"Ooh. Another mystery?" Wendy had been involved in one of their first mysteries, which had revolved around a quilt sewn during the Civil War. Tess decided to keep her response vague.

"Something like that."

"Well, I'm afraid I can't help you," Wendy said. "I haven't seen him. But I'll let you know if I do."

"Thank you." Tess turned to head back out.

Next up on her list was Antoinette's Closet, a vintage clothing store. Tess walked to the shop quickly, and as soon as she stepped in, Emma called out from behind the counter. "Hello, Mrs. Wallace."

"Hi, Emma."

"Are you looking for anything in particular today? We have a fun new dress that would look stunning on you." Emma pointed toward the front of the store, where a mannequin was wearing a long silky strapless sheath in a fire-truck red.

"It's been many years since I could pull something like that off." Tess laughed. "But God bless you for suggesting it."

"You'll never know unless you try," Emma said. Easy for her to say. She was probably a size 2, and young enough that fashion was still exciting for her.

"I think I'll spare the world that particular vision," Tess said. "Though I do love that purse." She pointed behind the counter, where a black leather clutch hung on a hook.

"Would you like to take a look at it?" Emma popped up to get it.

"No, I probably shouldn't," Tess said. Maybe another day. Today, she was on a mission. "I was actually hoping you could tell me whether you've seen this man or not." She held out her phone and showed her the photo.

"I'm afraid not," Emma said. Her long black hair swished as she shook her head.

"If you do see him, would you let me know?"

"Of course. And I'll just set that purse aside in case you come back." Emma grinned at her.

Tess laughed and headed out. Next she visited McHappy's Donuts, Bar-B-Cutie, Vance Hardware, and the Rivertown Grill. She also knocked on a few doors of the houses in the downtown area. She finally returned to the inn a couple of hours later, defeated.

She realized she should probably get dinner going, so she started browning hamburger and onions for a big, comforting pot of chili. She didn't think she would be able to eat much, she was so nervous about what they were about to do that night. What would happen out there on the bridge? Would they get the treasure back? Would they be in danger?

She'd drained the hamburger and was adding the spices, tomatoes, and beans just as Janice got back.

"Any luck? Tess asked.

"No. I went to a dozen places, but no one had seen him." Janice set her purse down with a thump. "I had such high hopes for the Antique and Salvage Mall too. I thought, if he might have picked the thing up at a thrift store, that's exactly the kind of place he'd hang out. But Harry said he's never seen the guy before."

"I had the same result," Tess said. "Not even a hint of recognition anywhere."

"It's like he wasn't even here. Are we the only ones who saw him?"

"He left the inn every day. Someone around here had to have seen him."

Janice nodded and looked over at the stove. "What are you making?"

"Chili. There's enough for an army."

"Mm-hmm." Janice's response was indecipherable at first. "I'm not sure I could eat anything."

"You have to eat something."

Janice sighed. "Maybe I'll just have a bowl of cereal."

That's when Tess realized that Janice was as nervous as she was. More, probably, considering she was more nervous by nature. Tess knew better than to push her, and she set the table while the chili simmered. She'd just finished up when LuAnn came into the common area. Tess could tell with one look that she'd had a very different experience than she and Janice had. Her eyes were bright, her cheeks pink, and she was bouncing up and down a bit—in excitement?

"They saw him. At Jeremiah's Coffee," LuAnn said.

There was a pause while they absorbed that news.

"So we're not crazy, then," Janice said.

"We're not crazy. Apparently he spent a good chunk of both Monday and Tuesday there. Several of the baristas remembered him well, because he spent many hours there enjoying the free wifi, nursing one cup of plain coffee. And he didn't even leave a tip."

"Do they have any idea who he is?" Tess asked.

"One of the baristas, Heather, says that she introduced herself, and he told her his name was Sawyer."

Tess blew out a breath. "Like Tom Sawyer?"

"Another fake name," Janice said.

"Most likely," LuAnn said. "Apparently he paid in cash, so there were no credit card receipts to track."

"So they have no idea who he is either?" Tess asked. She was so sure someone had to know who he was.

"I didn't say that." She glanced over at the stove. "Ooh. Chili?"

Tess nodded. "I'll dish it up. Now what do you mean? Do they know who he is or not?"

"Well, you know that one barista, Micah? The one with the stud in his chin?"

Tess had met him once or twice. He looked like a college kid, but with some extra hardware in his face.

"It just seems so unsanitary," Janice said.

LuAnn ignored her comment. "It turns out he's a computer science major at Marietta College. And he was curious about the guy who sat there all day and bought a two-dollar cup of coffee and didn't even leave a tip. So he used his computer science magic to figure out who he is."

LuAnn was leaving out a couple of steps there. "Huh?"

LuAnn sighed. "I don't remember exactly. It was something about wifi and something called a MAC address. What it boils down to is this: I guess every computer has its own number, and when he accessed the café's wifi, they were able to see the number of his computer. And then once they had the computer's number—"

"The MAC address?" Janice asked.

"Yeah, whatever it is." LuAnn waved her hand, as if the details were unimportant. "So anyway, Micah was able to use the MAC address to figure out what sites the guy had visited, and that allowed Micah to figure out who he is."

"And...?" Tess gestured for her to get to the punch line.

"His name is Russell Marchese. He lives in Parkersburg, West Virginia."

"Oh wow."

With that information, it wouldn't take them long at all to learn more about him.

"But get this. Micah was also able to find out something very interesting."

Tess had thought finding his real name was pretty interesting, but gestured for her to continue.

"Russell didn't just visit social media sites while he was at the coffee shop. You'll never guess what site he visited."

"What? Spit it out," Janice said.

LuAnn told them.

And Tess realized knowing it changed everything.

Chapter Twenty

July 25, 1863

Mr. Siloam handed Prudence an envelope when she arrived at Riverfront House the next morning.

"A guest left this for you," he said. "He asked me to hand it to you directly, and to make sure it did not leave my hands until it touched yours. He was very insistent about that."

Prudence held her breath. It was Mr. Clemens. It had to be from him. She took the envelope tentatively. Mr. Siloam was watching her, eyebrow cocked.

"Thank you," she said, and slipped the envelope into her pocket.

"Is..." He coughed. "Is everything all right?"

They both knew how unusual it was for a guest to leave anything for her.

"Yes," she said. She should probably explain what had happened. Mr. Siloam was at risk now too. They all were. But she couldn't seem to find the words. She smiled to reassure him. "Everything is fine."

The thing was, she felt, deep down in her spirit, that it *was* going to be all right. She didn't know anything about this Mr. Clemens, but something told her he could be trusted. He would be true to his word. He wouldn't tell.

Everything in her wanted to grasp the letter and read it immediately, but she had to act as if everything was normal, or Mr. Siloam would suspect something. She picked up a feather duster and moved into the parlor to clean. Mr. Siloam watched her, like he was trying to make up his mind about something, but she pretended she didn't notice and ran the feather duster over the top of the spinet.

She loved this room, with its rich flocked wallpaper and its velvet-covered armchairs. There was a sideboard carved with the most delicate flowers, and the beautifully done portrait of Governor John Brough above the fireplace. Light streamed in through the thick glass panes in the parlor window.

Finally, Mr. Siloam turned and followed after Elizabeth, who was headed into the kitchen. When Prudence was certain he was gone and no one was watching, she ducked into an alcove and pulled the envelope out of her pocket. Her hands shook as she unfolded the creamy paper.

Mrs. Willard,

I know you do not know whether to trust my intentions, and I do not blame you. I would not trust a stranger myself, not with so much at stake. But I hope that you will believe me when I say I was moved by what I saw, and that I want to help.

I am not brave like you, and cannot see a way for me to do much to help directly. I am not a man of means, and I fear I am not the kind of man whose prayers rise above the ceiling. But I will find a way to help your cause; more than that, I will find a way, someday, to make sure you are rewarded for the risks you take on behalf of those in need.

My address is below. I pray you will keep in touch and let me know if there is anything you need or any way I can help now.

Yours,
Samuel L. Clemens

Prudence read the letter over twice. She didn't know what to make of it. Surely this Mr. Clemens couldn't think that she would write back, that she would keep him abreast of the happenings here at Riverfront House and the deliveries she received. Was he mad?

But there was something genuine in his words too. Something earnest. She believed that he really did want to help. That he really did believe he would find a way to thank her someday. It was kind, but she wasn't involved in this because she wanted thanks or any sort of reward. The best way he could help was by keeping his mouth closed about what he'd witnessed.

But, she thought as she slipped the letter back into her pocket, there was something she wanted to say to him. As she ran her feather duster over the wooden bench by the spinet, she thought about what he'd said about not being the sort of man whose prayers rise above the ceiling.

That could not be. God listened to the prayers of all who called on His name. The prayers of His children were precious to the Lord. Could Mr. Clemens really believe God didn't listen?

Prudence decided she would write back to Mr. Clemens after all. She would tell him that the best thing he could do to help their cause was to believe that the good Lord loved him and listened when he prayed. She would tell him that the best way he could help would be to ask for the Lord's protection over their endeavors.

She would tell him, and see how he chose to respond. What happened after that would be up to him.

Chapter Twenty-One

"I can't believe we're doing this," Tess said as she stepped onto the Harmar Bridge that night. The sky had clouded over, with thick heavy clouds rolling in as the day waned, and the night was dark. The old railroad bridge crossed the Muskingum River and linked old Harmar Village to the main town of Marietta. The trestles had long been removed from the bed of the bridge, but a wooden pedestrian walkway had been built just to the side of where the tracks had been, supported by the iron girders and the cement pilings. It was a quaint old bridge, charming for a stroll on a summer day or in peak foliage season. But on this cloudy November night, it was just dark and spooky.

Janice and LuAnn waited at the base of the bridge, by the docks of the Marietta Harbor. The whole area, which was usually busy with boaters tying up sailboats and ski boats in summer, was deserted tonight.

Tess hovered at the edge of the walkway, keeping to the shadows, and Brad waited at the far end, on the Harmar end. He'd been glad to accompany them—had insisted he would have been upset if they hadn't asked him, in fact. Tess knew they all felt better having him there.

Moses was now making his way down the narrow wooden plankway toward the middle of the bridge. She saw his dark figure, but nothing else moved. It was just past nine. Would Isaiah—Russell—show after all?

It felt strange to think of him as Russell, but now they not only knew his name and home address, they also knew that he was an electrician, was married, and that his house was about to be repossessed by the bank. It had only taken about a half hour of scanning social media and public records in Parkersburg to find all that out. Tess couldn't even imagine what they would've uncovered if they'd had more time. But she felt better that going into this, she knew who he really was and why he wanted to sell the treasure so badly.

If he really *had* the treasure, she reminded herself. But given his search history at the coffee shop, she felt fairly certain he not only had it, but knew that $50,000 was a bargain for the object he had in his possession. Whatever happened tonight, they had to get that treasure. It was... Tess shook her head.

It was priceless.

There was a noise at the far end of the bridge. She saw Moses stiffen, and then she heard footsteps. She held her breath, waiting. She had her phone out, ready to call for help if this went badly.

Out of the shadows, a form slowly took shape. It was Russell, all right. He wore a wide-brimmed hat, but Tess recognized his stocky frame. He had a backpack slung over one shoulder.

The men greeted each other by bobbing their heads. Neither said a word.

"Did you bring the check?" Russell's voice carried over the water on this still night. He had more of a drawl than he'd displayed when he stayed at the inn.

"I have a check right here." Moses pulled an envelope out of his pocket. "Do you have it? The treasure?"

Russell nodded. "The check first."

"I want some answers first," said Moses. "I think I deserve that much."

There was a long pause. Then finally Russell spoke. "What do you want to know?"

"How did you get it?" Moses asked.

"You'd be amazed what you can find poking around junk shops. My wife found it there. She just liked the box it came in. But when I did some research, I found out what it really was. When I read how much it would be worth, well, I realized we had something very special on our hands."

"How did you find me? How did you know it was rightfully mine?"

"Well, I got lucky, didn't I? When a family uses the same name through five generations it's pretty easy to follow the thread."

"And your name?"

"I thought that was pretty clever. When I found out you use a pen name, I couldn't resist the irony. Now, enough with the twenty questions. Where's my check?"

Moses took a deep breath and handed the envelope to him.

Russell slid his finger under the flap of the envelope and withdrew a thin white piece of paper.

Tess held her breath. Had Moses given him the real check? Or the lookalike? Would it even matter?

Russell pulled out his cell phone and used the flashlight function to light up the paper. Moses shifted his weight from foot to foot. *Please, Lord,* Tess prayed. *Let him hand over the treasure now.*

"This is fake," Russell said.

"What makes you say that?" Tess could hear the apprehension in Moses's voice. She figured Russell could hear it too.

She was right. "You're trying to cheat me," Russell growled.

"I won't cheat you," Moses said. His voice had taken on the soothing register of someone trying to calm an angry toddler. "Look. Why would I do that? I'm good for it. I just want the family heirloom back. I'm not trying to cheat anyone." He held up his hands. "But okay, I wanted a glimpse of the thing before I handed you the actual check. So let's see it, and I will give you this." He reached into his pocket and pulled out another envelope.

"You tried to cheat me," Russell said. He seemed incredulous. Could he really be shocked, Tess wondered, that someone hadn't played straight with him, after all he'd done? But she kept her mouth shut and prayed once again that God would make everything work out.

"Let's see it." Moses lifted his chin. "How do I know what you really have in that backpack? How do I know it's anything at all?"

"You think you can just order me around? Try to swindle me, and I'll roll over?"

"I just want to see it." Moses's voice took on a growing urgency.

"Hand over the real check."

"Not until you show me what's in that backpack."

Tess held her breath. *Just give him the check,* she thought. What did $50,000 matter? Then again, it wasn't her money. If it was, making sure she got what she paid for would probably be of utmost importance to her too.

Russell swung the backpack around and unzipped it slowly. She could hear the teeth of the zipper unhook, one by one, in the quiet night.

"Take it out," Moses said. He still held the check in one hand.

Russell hesitated, and then opened the flap so Moses could see inside. Tess couldn't see what was in the backpack from here. She prayed it was what they thought it was.

Moses leaned forward to look, but as he did, Russell grabbed for the check. Moses stepped back just in time, and Russell shouted, "Give me that money!" The words echoed over the water.

"Not until I see what's in the backpack," Moses said calmly.

"You're cheating me." Russell's voice was getting higher, more breathless. This was not going the way he wanted it to. He was starting to spin out of control. "You can't cheat me. You hand me that check right now, or you'll be sorry."

"Let me see what's in the backpack." Moses's voice was calm, measured, which made Russell's rising hysteria all the more pronounced.

"Give me that check now," he shouted as he lunged forward again.

"I just want to see it," Moses said again, pulling his arm and the check back.

"You want to see it?" Russell was shaking now, Tess saw. She wasn't sure how he'd managed to pass himself off as a stable businessman at the inn; tonight it was clear there was something unhinged about him. "You want to see it?"

Moses waited.

"Hand me the check now, or you will never see this treasure."

Moses crossed his arms over his chest, the envelope containing the real check still clutched in one hand.

Why wouldn't Russell just show Moses what was in the backpack? Tess wondered. Was it because there wasn't really anything there?

Russell took the backpack off and held it by the strap. "I'll drop it over the side." He held his arm out, so the backpack dangled over the water.

Tess sucked in a breath. If he dropped it into the water... She didn't even want to think about what would be lost.

Everything in her wanted to rush out onto the bridge to grab the backpack, but she had a feeling any interference at this point would push Russell over the edge.

"I just want to see—"

"And I just want the money!" Russell screamed it, his face screwed up with anger. "You have until I count to three, and then it will be too late. One..."

Moses didn't move. Was Russell really going to do it? He wouldn't be that crazy, would he?

"Two..."

But then, this whole thing was crazy. The whole plot—from the note in the mail to the meeting on the bridge—was evidence that something was not quite right with Russell. There was an air of desperation that defied all logic. If he really had the treasure, why didn't he go through a more traditional way to profit from it? Surely he would have found a buyer, if they were right about what was inside that bag. Which raised the question, what really was inside that bag? Why had he targeted Moses specifically? Why would he do it this way?

Her thoughts came to a crashing halt as Russell calmly said, "Three," and let go of the backpack.

"No!" she shouted before she could stop herself. If there was any chance it really was—if he'd just destroyed—

Russell's head jerked toward her.

"Who's here?" he shouted, and started rushing toward her.

Moses blocked him, but Russell pushed past him. Tess knew she should turn, knew she should run, but she was frozen, listening for the backpack to hit the water. She almost fainted when she heard the splash.

"Run! Tess, go!" Moses called, and Tess realized she only had seconds. She turned and ran, her footsteps pounding against the wooden walkway until she made it off the approach and headed down toward the grass, toward the docks.

Her heart pounded, filling her ears, and she prayed that Plan B was already in motion, though she couldn't see it. She saw LuAnn scrambling over the giant rocks at the base of the bridge, heading for the river. Janice was just a few steps behind.

Tess rushed toward them. She heard a noise at the end of the bridge and looked up. There was Chief Nelson Mayfield, coming out of the woods on the other side of the bridge, just about to step into the walkway, blocking Russell's exit. "Stop right there." His deep voice boomed.

Brad had insisted on alerting the police. He was happy to help, but only if they got Chief Mayfield involved. He'd called the police chief himself, saying it would be lunacy for the four of them to head out tonight without some police backup. Moses hadn't liked the idea, but Brad gave them no choice, and right about now, Tess was glad he hadn't.

Chief Mayfield had Russell under control, so she turned her attention to LuAnn, who was already wading into the river. What was she going to—

And then she saw the backpack, bobbing on the surface of the water. It hadn't sunk. There was still a chance—

"LuAnn! Don't—"

But LuAnn was already waist-deep in the water, stretching to reach the dark parcel as the current carried it past.

"Be careful!" Janice called. She stepped out to the edge of the rocks and held out her hand.

Oh Lord, please keep her safe, Tess prayed. The Muskingum River wasn't all that wide, but they were only yards away from where it joined the Ohio River, and the eddies and currents at the junction could be strong and unpredictable. If LuAnn were to lose her footing—

And wearing that heavy coat—

Tess couldn't watch.

"I got it!" LuAnn was chest-deep in the frigid river, but she had grabbed the backpack and was carefully making her way back to the rocks. Janice and Tess both reached out and hauled her back onto land on her knees.

"I'm fine," she said, standing up. "We got it. We just—see if it's all right."

Tess didn't see how it could have survived, not after being submerged in the river. Even if that backpack really contained what they hoped, it was surely ruined now. Lost forever.

Tess picked up the backpack and water poured out, while Janice took off her own coat and wrapped it around LuAnn's shoulders. Tess hoisted the bag by the strap. It was heavy. It seemed too heavy. Maybe that was because it was wet? The women made it back to the grass and climbed up to the walkway where Moses and Chief Mayfield had restrained Russell and where Brad was just reaching their side of the bridge.

Tess set the backpack on the ground and knelt beside it. Janice and LuAnn crouched down next to her. Janice pulled her phone out and turned the flashlight on. The light reflected against something shiny.

"There's a bag." Tess's words came out in a rush. "A plastic bag."

Tess reached in and pulled out a wooden box, encased in a heavy plastic bag.

"It looks old," LuAnn breathed.

"It also looks dry." Tess's hands were shaking, but she did her best to steady them and unzip the plastic seal on the bag. She got it open and pulled out the box. It was a little over a foot long, almost as wide, maybe eight inches deep, and built of simple, sturdy oak. There was no decoration or mark of any kind. It was exactly the kind of box Prudence would have appreciated. The wood was scarred but the box was finely crafted, and it took Tess a moment to figure out how to open the brass catch that held it closed.

Finally, she nudged it open and lifted the box's lid. Inside was a stack of papers, snugly held together with a brown ribbon.

Tess recognized the first page immediately. It was the note that had been in the picture Russell had texted as proof that he had the treasure.

Tess carefully untied the ribbon and lifted that page out.

When they saw what was written on the paper underneath, LuAnn let out a shout, and Janice fell back and sat on the grass.

But Tess just stared at the words. She couldn't be reading that right.

But she was. After all this time, they'd really found it.

Chapter Twenty-Two

Half an hour later, they were all seated around a roaring fire in the inn's lobby, but Tess still hadn't gotten over the shock.

Moses held the box on his lap. He'd been gently turning the yellowed pages the last ten minutes, trying to make out the spidery blue handwriting. He was undoubtedly trying to take in the magnitude of what he held in his hands.

The Adventures of Huck and Jim, the title page read. *By Mark Twain.*

"So this is...what?" Sharon asked. "A sequel? To *The Adventures of Huckleberry Finn?*"

LuAnn had changed into dry clothes, but she still sat closest to the fire with a blanket around her shoulders. Brad sat next to her on the couch, snuggled up just a bit too close for either one to deny it was accident, Tess thought. LuAnn's teeth were still chattering a bit when she started to explain.

"*The Adventures of Huckleberry Finn* was published in 1884, and quickly became a best seller," she explained. "If you remember, that book ends with Huck determined to run away again. "So Twain started working on a sequel soon afterward."

Tess grabbed the copy of *The Adventures of Huckleberry Finn* they'd pulled off the inn's bookshelves, flipped to the last page, and read the novel's famous last words. "'But I reckon I got to light out for the territory ahead of the rest, because Aunt Sally she's going to adopt me and sivilize me, and I can't stand it. I been there before.'"

"You said Twain wrote a couple of books where Huck and Tom have other adventures after that," Tess said.

"That's right." LuAnn nodded. "And there were a couple of unfinished sequels as well. The most well-known fragment has Huck Finn and Tom Sawyer and Jim heading west on the trail of two girls kidnapped by Sioux Indians."

"But he never finished it, right?" Janice held a mug of peppermint tea, warming her face with the steam wafting from it.

"Right. He abandoned that sequel fifteen thousand words in," LuAnn confirmed.

"You said it was eventually published, though," Tess said.

LuAnn pulled the blanket a bit tighter around her. Her lips were starting to look just a bit less blue.

"All of his known unfinished works have been published," she said.

"Why did he stop writing that sequel?" Janice asked.

LuAnn shrugged. "No one is sure."

"Maybe he thought it wasn't any good," Sharon said.

"Maybe," LuAnn said. "But there has always been speculation that he abandoned the sequel because he started another version."

"A different sequel?" Janice asked.

LuAnn nodded. "But like I said, it has always been speculation. No one ever knew for sure if it existed. Until now, that is."

"Until now." Moses's tone was reverent, and he turned the pages gently.

"So you think this is the lost sequel, the one he abandoned the Sioux one to write?" Brad asked.

"I'm certain of it," Moses said. There were tears in his eyes.

"It will need to be verified, I'm sure," Tess said. She didn't want to crush his hopes, but surely the experts would want to examine it and make that determination.

"I'm sure it will." Moses smiled, turning the paper gently. "But I don't need an expert to tell me why there's a woman named Prudence in this story."

"What? Really?" Tess hadn't examined the pages carefully, but Moses had been studying them for a while now.

"Really." Moses wiped his eyes. "And it appears to be complete. From what I can make out, this is a very different kind of story than the other attempt at a sequel. In the little bit I've read, Jim and Huck keep heading north along the Ohio River, and they finally make it to Ohio."

"No way," Janice breathed.

Tess tried to understand. He couldn't possibly mean—

"In this first chapter, they run into a number of people who want to send Jim back down south, but they get away, and finally, they are directed to a woman who can help get Jim to safety."

"And this woman is—"

"Named Prudence," Moses confirmed. "She works at a place called the Riverfront House."

"Oh my." Tess tried to wrap her head around this.

"Obviously we'll need to keep reading to see what happens, but I have a suspicion I know why Twain gave it to them," Moses said.

"He wrote them into the sequel as a way of honoring what they did," Janice said softly.

"But why wouldn't they go ahead and publish it?" Tess asked. "I mean, it's an honor to have Mark Twain write you into a book, but what good is it unless it actually gets published? No one ever knows about it."

They were quiet for a minute, thinking. The fire popped and a log settled. Then LuAnn said, "Think about Prudence's diary entry. She said its very existence put them at risk."

"Maybe Prudence and Jason would have gotten in trouble if anyone found out about the slaves they'd helped," Brad said.

"But this was, what, more than twenty years later?" Janice said. "How could they still get in trouble twenty years later?"

"I don't think they could have gotten into legal trouble," LuAnn said, "but I can imagine that after Prudence and Jason had lived for so many years with the fear of discovery, they would never have thought that worldly riches were more valuable than the safety of their family. I don't think they would have taken the chance that there wasn't someone out there who would come after them after all those years. Not publishing was the safest choice to make."

"But it was still a very valuable gift," Sharon said. "The letter that came with it seemed to give them ownership of the book free and clear. I assume that means they owned the copyright. So if at any point they wanted to publish it, they could have."

"Copyrights worked differently back then," Moses said. "But essentially, yes, the way I read that note, they could have had the book published and kept the proceeds."

"Amazing," Janice said, shaking her head. "What an incredibly generous gift."

"A finished sequel to *Huckleberry Finn* would have been a big best seller," Tess said.

"But they chose not to publish it," Moses said, shaking his head. "It's incredible, thinking how our family's story might have been different if they had."

Tess could only imagine. That money could have changed everything for Moses's ancestors. College, real estate, security. It was hard to imagine passing all that up.

Then again, its very existence and the secrets it revealed could have taken everything from them as well.

Tess realized that Moses was now in a position to make the same decision his ancestors had. Would this book ever see the light of day? Would the world ever know that a lost manuscript by one of the nation's greatest writers had been discovered? Moses had a lot of thinking to do.

"But why wouldn't Russell have just published it?" LuAnn said.

Before he'd been carted off by Chief Mayfield, Russell had explained that his wife had found the box at a thrift store and brought it home, not realizing what was inside. He'd recognized right away that they had something valuable on their hands, and set about tracking down a way to offload it for cash. Tess wasn't sure the police would be able to charge him with anything they could make stick, but at least he was far away from them and the manuscript.

"Most likely because he realized the ownership of such a thing would be murky and hotly contested," Brad said.

"Wouldn't this book be in the public domain?" Moses asked. "I thought that anything published before 1923 is now in the public domain."

"Anything *published* by 1923 is," Brad said. "But this hasn't been published, so it doesn't qualify. I did a bit of research about it after you all told me what you thought the treasure was. If this book had been published before that cutoff date, it would be free and clear for anyone to use. But in 1962, the University of California acquired the right to all *unpublished* Twain material. So if our thief did even a tiny bit of research on the manuscript, he would have quickly discovered that he wouldn't be able to profit on this at all; the manuscript would be owned by the university."

"Which must be why he tried to find a private buyer," Sharon said.

"And he used the letter that came with the manuscript to see who it had been sent to originally. It couldn't have been hard to find Moses Willard, the descendant, of, well, a long line of Moses Willards."

It all made sense, in a twisted, sad sort of way.

"So you won't make anything from it if you publish it now?" Janice asked Moses.

"I don't know, and honestly, it doesn't really matter. This is not about money. I'll have to think about what to do."

"You mean, there's a chance you *wouldn't* have it published?" LuAnn seemed incredulous. "Even if you wouldn't get to make anything from it, you're holding a national treasure in your hands. Why would you keep it to yourself?"

Moses shrugged. "I'm not saying I will. I'm just saying, my family kept its existence quiet for many generations, even into the 1920s, when Prudence and Jason were long dead and the danger had passed. Maybe there's a reason. I guess I just need to pray about it and ask the Lord for guidance and wisdom."

At the end of the day, it was the Willard family's secret to keep, or to share. Tess didn't envy Moses having to choose between his family legacy and an unknown work by a beloved author, but she knew that he would be wise and thoughtful in his decision. At the very least, the treasure was now back where it belonged—with a descendant of Prudence and Jason.

Tess couldn't help but think Prudence would be proud to see her great-great-great-grandson here, his wife beside him, his children sleeping upstairs. She would be proud of how kind he was, and how thoughtful, and talented. And she would be deeply honored to know that the faith that had sustained her through everything she'd endured, through the dangers and the trials and the heartache, had been passed down through the generations and still inspired the members of her family all these years later.

That was the greatest legacy of all. To see your children and grandchildren grow into their own faith, to trust God with their own trials and challenges and joys. Looking around this cheerful, cozy inn now, Tess couldn't be more thankful for the lineage of faithful men and women who had passed their love for the Lord down to her. And she was so grateful for her own children, and the families they were starting.

Tess closed her eyes for a moment. Yes, seeing her daughter with her kids was one of the greatest joys of her life. Something she couldn't imagine going without.

Tess sighed. She realized there was something she needed to do. She would go talk to Lizzie.

Tonight, though—tonight she would sit a little longer with these people who had become like family, and bask in the warm glow of the fire and the knowledge that they'd solved another mystery.

CHAPTER TWENTY-THREE

Tess took a deep breath before she knocked on the door. She heard voices inside, and what sounded like a hundred pairs of feet rushing around. Finally, she let out her breath, ran through what she wanted to say one more time, and pressed the doorbell.

"Just a minute!" The door flew open, and Lizzie stood there in sweats and an oversized T-shirt.

"Oh. Hi, Mom." She seemed more surprised than upset, Tess thought. That was promising.

"We're going out through the garage!" Michael yelled from inside, and Tess could see him herding one, two, three little bodies into the garage.

"It looks like I've stopped by at a bad time," Tess said.

"No, not at all." Lizzie stepped back and waved her in. "Just your typical Saturday morning chaos. Michael is taking the boys to their karate lesson and Harper to her ballet class. This is the quietest this house is going to get all day. Come on in."

Lizzie and Michael had bought a cute bungalow in Marietta when they were ready to start a family. She'd spent many years decorating it just to her liking, sanding down the original white oak floors and restaining them, installing a kitchen with marble counters and stainless steel appliances, and spending hours choosing between various shades of white for the walls. Now, three kids later, the home was still gorgeous but also usually crowded with balls and discarded sweaters and lone sneakers and dolls in various states of dress. The fridge was covered with finger paintings, and there were three different kinds of cereal sitting out on the counter.

"Sorry for the mess. It's been a long week."

"No need to apologize." There was a tension in the air, but Tess decided to plow on ahead. "I brought that platter you wanted." She held out the shopping bag she had over her arm. The platter was wrapped in dish towels inside.

"Thank you," Lizzie said. She took the bag and set it on the counter. "But I'm guessing you didn't drive all the way out here to bring me a platter."

"No, not exactly."

"Have a seat." Lizzie gestured at the table. "Coffee?"

"Sure."

Lizzie poured them both cups from the pot on the counter and stirred in milk and sugar. Then she sat down across the table from her mom.

"I wanted to talk to you about Thanksgiving," Tess began.

"Me too," Lizzie said. "I've been praying and spending a lot of time talking to God about this, and I think I'm finally starting to understand why you wanted to do your own thing this year. It's still not what I would choose, but I wanted to say I'm sorry for not being more supportive of your decision."

"My...what?" Tess couldn't have heard that right.

"Your decision to have Thanksgiving at the inn instead of here," Lizzie said. "I'm not gonna lie, at first I was kind of hurt by it, especially with Jeff Jr. away this year. But I know you have a business to run, and your friends, and I can see why it's hard for you to get away. And I can see why it would be kind of fun to celebrate with your friends you've known forever."

"What?" Tess felt like an idiot repeating herself, but she wasn't sure what else to say. Was she totally misunderstanding what Lizzie was getting at? Or was this really what Lizzie thought had happened here? "Are you saying you think I chose to have Thanksgiving at the inn instead of here with you?"

Lizzie nodded. "And again, I get it. I—"

"Lizzie. I thought you didn't want me here."

"What?" Lizzie's eyes widened. "What in the world made you think that?"

"Because you kept talking about how crazy it was going to be with Michael's family here, and you said you wouldn't have room for me."

"I did not say that. I would never—"

"It's okay, honey. I understand. I really do."

"But Mom." Lizzie shook her head. "That's not at all what I was thinking. I *want* you to come. Of course I want you here. I never said I didn't want you."

But she had, hadn't she? Maybe those exact words hadn't come out of her mouth, but that's what she meant.

"But it was going to be too crazy with all those people."

"There *will* be a lot of people here. But the one person I can always count on to actually help is you."

Tess felt tears prick her eyes. "Really?"

"Of course." Lizzie took a sip of her coffee. "I don't know how I managed to give you the idea that you weren't welcome, but nothing could be further from the truth. I would love it if you came for Thanksgiving."

"Truly?"

"Really, Mom."

Tess lifted her own coffee cup and took a sip, trying to make sense of this. How had she gotten things so backward?

"*Could* you come? I mean, at this point? It sounded like you were pretty far into the planning for the dinner at the inn."

That was true. It would be terribly selfish to leave LuAnn in the lurch. Was it too late to back out of that now?

But then she thought back to her talk with LuAnn. LuAnn had encouraged her to talk to Lizzie. She'd known what Tess really wanted. She'd been planning on hosting the dinner with or without her help.

"I'll have to talk to LuAnn to make sure I wouldn't be making things harder for her. But I'm fairly certain she'll say I should come here. And if she does, I would love to."

"I would love that too," Lizzie said. She shook her head. "Goodness, Mom. I can't believe I made you think you weren't welcome here. You're always welcome. Please know that."

"But you do have Michael's entire family coming to join you..." Tess said.

"Exactly why I need backup. His mom will spend the whole time talking about what a perfect child he was—implying I should be doing a better job with my own children—and his dad will spend the whole time trying to talk to me about my retirement plan. It drives me batty."

Tess laughed, but she felt bad about it. "So you don't prefer them after all, then?"

"Oh for Pete's sake, Mom." Lizzie let out a long sigh. "You cannot tell me you actually thought that."

Tess shrugged. "They seem like good people."

"His parents are nice." Lizzie thought for a minute, as if choosing her next words carefully. "I can't complain, really. It's just that they're not my family, you know? They have different traditions, and inside jokes I don't get, and, I don't know." She went quiet for a minute. "I guess, especially since Dad passed away, I just want to be around *my* family, you know?"

Tess nodded as the tears spilled over. She knew. She very much knew. Her family had always been the most important thing to her. But since Jeffrey died, it seemed in some ways more important than ever.

"I want that too," Tess said. And then, when Lizzie got up and grabbed tissues for them, she joked, "At least, most of the time. There's only so many times even a doting grandma can read *The Book With No Pictures* before going a little crazy."

"I suppose that's true." Lizzie laughed. "Thank you, Mom."

"For what?"

"For coming over to talk about this. I—" She closed her eyes for a moment, and then shook her head and continued. "I knew you were upset about something, but I didn't have the slightest idea what. And it would have been terrible to miss

Thanksgiving because of a misunderstanding. Please know that you are always welcome here, no matter what."

Tess didn't say anything for a moment. She watched the small curls of steam rise off her cup. And then she smiled.

"Thank you, Lizzie. You and your family and your brother are the most important thing in my world." And then, a beat later, she added, "Well, and coffee. You, your family, your brother, and coffee."

Lizzie laughed. "You really can't make it through a sweet moment without a joke, can you?"

"I suppose I can't," Tess said. "But it doesn't mean I don't mean it. Not the coffee part, but the rest of it."

"Oh, you absolutely do mean the coffee part," Lizzie said, but she was still laughing. "It's okay, Mom. Your sense of humor is part of what makes you you. And that's just fine by me." She took a sip of her coffee. "Family really is the most important thing."

Tess smiled and nodded without saying a word. Thanksgiving was coming, and with it came opportunities to love and to serve and to focus on her blessings.

Sitting here in her daughter's home, surrounded by reminders of the people who made her heart swell with a love she'd never imagined—this was what mattered.

Thank You, Lord, she prayed. *I have so much to be thankful for.*

Dear Reader,

I couldn't believe my luck when I was asked to collaborate with E. E. (Ellen) Kennedy on a story involving Mark Twain. Mark Twain, one of the heroes of American literature and one of the most charismatic and complicated figures in letters?! I was in! But even though I'd read most of his books (English major here), once I started to really dig into this story, I realized how little I really knew about his life. I had known that he was against slavery (that's pretty clear if you read *The Adventures of Huckleberry Finn*), but I hadn't realized his feelings about Native Americans were more complicated. I knew he'd married, but I hadn't realized how the death of his daughter had devastated his family. I hadn't realized he'd started many attempts at sequels to *The Adventures of Tom Sawyer* and *The Adventures of Huckleberry Finn*. There was plenty to work with as a jumping off point for a story.

While I loved getting the chance to learn more about Twain as I wrote, I also enjoyed getting to know the characters of LuAnn, Tess, and Janice a bit more, and it was fun to imagine how each of them would react to the search for the missing Twain treasure.

As far as I know, there are no undiscovered Mark Twain manuscripts out there waiting to be discovered... but who knows? There are a lot of boxes in a lot of attics in this country. Isn't it fun to imagine *what if*?

I would especially like to acknowledge Ellen Kennedy and offer special thanks for her hard work and creative ingenuity in coming up with such a fun story idea.

Happy reading,
Beth Adams

About the Authors

Beth Adams lives in Brooklyn, New York, with her husband and two young daughters. When she's not writing, she spends her time cleaning up after two devious cats and trying to find time to read mysteries.

E. E. (Ellen) Kennedy is the author of the Miss Prentice Cozy Mystery Series.

Marietta's Harmar Bridge

The pivotal scene in this book takes place on the historic Harmar Bridge, an old railroad bridge that spans the Muskingum River and connects historic Harmar Village with Marietta proper. Harmar Village is listed on the National Register of Historic Places, and is a quaint area with shops, restaurants, historic buildings, and brick streets.

The first bridge across this span of river, a covered bridge, was built in 1856. It was destroyed in the flood of 1913, and replaced by an 826-foot rotating railroad bridge—a term I had to look up! The span actually swings open, rotating 90 degrees to allow boats to pass through, and then swings closed, reconnecting the two banks of the river. It is the oldest operating swing bridge in the country and is not mechanized—it operates entirely by manpower! The bridge is opened each year during the Harmar Days festival in July.

Harmar Bridge was converted to a pedestrian bridge in 1962, and today you can stroll across the walkway and experience this piece of Ohio history.

Something Delicious from our Wayfarers Inn Friends

LuAnn's Butternut Squash Lasagna with Nutmeg Béchamel Sauce

For the vegetables:
- 1 medium butternut squash, peeled, seeded, and cut into ½ inch cubes
- 2 Tablespoons olive oil
- Kosher salt
- 1 small onion, sliced

For the béchamel sauce:
- 4 Tablespoons unsalted butter
- 4 Tablespoons all-purpose flour
- 4 cups whole milk
- 1 teaspoon freshly grated nutmeg

For the lasagna:
- Butter for the dish
- 1 cup grated mozzarella cheese
- 1 cup grated parmesan cheese
- 1 package no-boil lasagna noodles

Preheat oven to 425 degrees. Toss the squash with one tablespoon of the olive oil and a pinch of salt, and set in the oven. Toss the sliced onion with the other tablespoon of olive oil and some more salt, and set on another rack in the oven. Roast for 18–20 minutes, keeping an eye on the vegetables so they don't burn. When the vegetables are soft, take out of the oven and set aside and lower the temperature to 350 degrees.

While the vegetables are cooking, make the béchamel sauce. Melt the butter in a medium saucepan over medium heat. Whisk in the flour until smooth, and cook, whisking the whole time, until the flour is lightly golden but not brown, about 2 minutes. Gradually whisk in the milk, a little at a time, until smooth. Bring to a boil, then reduce the heat to medium low and simmer, stirring occasionally, until thickened, about 5 minutes. Stir in the nutmeg and take off the heat.

Butter a 9 × 13-inch baking dish. Spread about a quarter of the béchamel on the bottom of the baking dish and top with noodles. Spread more béchamel, and top with half the vegetables and a third of the cheeses. Add another layer of noodles, more béchamel, the remaining vegetables, and a third of the cheese. Add one more layer of noodles and top with the rest of the béchamel and the rest of the cheese. Loosely cover the dish with foil and bake for 45 minutes or until cooked through, and then remove foil and cook until the cheese browns.

Read on for a sneak peek of another exciting book in the Secrets of Wayfarers Inn series!

The Innkeepers' Conundrum
by Kim Vogel Sawyer

LuAnn gently twisted the glittering gold ribbons cascading from the bow at the top of the Christmas tree and directed them toward the thick bottom branches. She'd considered draping the tree in threads of tinsel, but when she spotted the gold topper with its array of four-inch-wide ribbons in the holiday section of a specialty shop in Canton, she'd changed her mind. Now she was glad for the choice. The half dozen falls of ribbon finished the tree perfectly.

Such a lovely tree, a towering ten feet tall and covered from top to bottom in ornaments similar to the ones her mother had hung on their Christmas trees when she was a child, including antique multi-colored reflector balls and mercury glass Santa Clauses, birds, pinecones, and stars. Of course, she couldn't cover a ten-foot tree with antique ornaments. Not without breaking the bank. But reproduction ornaments, purchased at a fraction of the price of genuine antiques, interspersed with shatterproof balls, teardrops, and onion-shaped ornaments, gave the old-world appearance she wanted.

Tess descended the stairs, her arms full of linens, and peeked over the railing at the tree. She whistled. "Wow, Lu, it looks fantastic. The prettiest of all of them."

"Thanks." LuAnn had insisted on putting seven-foot trees at the ends of the hallways on all levels, one in the café, and one in the library. Pint-sized trees decorated mantels, bathroom shelves, and the corner of the bar next to the antique cash register. But this one was definitely the pièce de résistance. It needed to be special since it was the one guests would see when they stepped through the front doors.

LuAnn eased backward several feet, perusing the tree with a critical eye. Ribbons evenly spaced. Ornaments strategically placed both at the branches' tips and closer to the tree's trunk, giving a 3-D effect. No empty gaps, except—

She darted forward, removed one teardrop-shaped ornament, and reaffixed it a scant half inch to the right. She angled her head, scowling, then nodded. The painted snowflake on a blue background now complemented rather than competed with a striped, oversized ball.

Tess came the rest of the way down the stairs and stopped next to LuAnn. "You really have outdone yourself with the decorating. Thanks for taking it on. I can't imagine the inn being any more festive."

Their first Christmas at Wayfarers Inn. Shouldn't it be extra special? LuAnn fluffed one of the gold ribbons. "I still need to clip on the bubble lights and LED candles on the tips of some of the branches, but now that I see the tree with the ornaments in place, I'm no longer disappointed about going with artificial." She tossed a grin over her shoulder. "I like being able to bend the branches to accommodate the placement of ornaments."

Tess shook her head. "You are such a perfectionist. Really, you need counseling." Her smile let LuAnn know she was teasing. She bounced the rumpled bundle spilling over her arms. There were piles of sheets and towels to wash after their full-capacity Thanksgiving week. "I better get these to the laundry room before Janice comes looking for me." She ambled through the foyer to the café and disappeared from view.

LuAnn pulled a string of liquid-filled bubble lights from the box next to the stairs and untangled them. Christmas… a time of peace and goodwill to men. A time when families gathered to celebrate Christ's birth, partake of traditional recipes, and exchange gifts. It should be a joyful time. So why did sadness pinch her chest? She didn't have to ponder long. For as far back as she could remember, Christmas meant being with Mom. Until this year.

The passage of months hadn't erased the dull ache of grief, but at least she wouldn't be alone, thanks to Tess and Janice and the scheduled guests. In fact, she'd be less alone than she'd ever been before. With no husband or children, her holiday gatherings had always been quiet and largely uneventful. With the exception of the year an ice storm brought down a tree limb on the power line to their house and they spent

Christmas day without electricity. A cold sandwich made a poor holiday dinner, but they'd bundled up in blankets and played checkers and Parcheesi by candlelight. A smile tugged at her lips. Funny how the day that had seemed so awful then now lingered as a precious memory.

She hummed "O Christmas Tree" while clipping on the bubble lights and the individual LED candles. When she finished, she knelt and plugged in the outlet strip. The tree lit up like...well, like a Christmas tree. Smiling, she stood with her hands on her hips and admired her handiwork. As soon as she put the Victorian crazy-quilt tree skirt into place and added a few empty boxes dressed in holiday paper and oversized bows, her decorating would be complete. She tapped her chin. Now, where had she put that tree skirt?

The lights on the tree flickered, the overhead chandelier strobed in off beats, and then with a *pop!*, the area went dark. LuAnn blinked in surprise. She almost ran to the window to see if a tree limb had taken out the power line, but the pendant lights in the café and the upstairs hallway lights hadn't gone out, so she must have blown a breaker. She huffed. Hadn't the electrician assured them the new wiring would handle the needs of the inn?

The front door opened, allowing in a chilly breeze, and their Realtor and friend, Brad Grimes, blew in with it. He pushed the door closed with his foot while balancing a sizable box against his stomach. He looked around, confusion marring his face. "Why's it so dark in here?"

LuAnn huffed again. "I blew a breaker. And I only plugged in one power strip." She plunked her fist on her hip. "That shouldn't happen with our new wiring, should it?"

He crossed to the bar-turned-reception desk and slid the box onto the top. "Hmm, that depends. How much amperage did you put on the power strip?"

She'd taught English and history to hundreds of students. She was not a stupid woman. But she had no idea how to answer his question. She flapped her hand at the tree. "Only what's on this."

Brad frowned at the tree, his gaze drifting from the fluffy gold ball of ribbon at the top all the way to the lowest branches. He fingered one of the now non-bubbling bubble lights. "How many of the little incandescent strings did you wind onto this tree?"

She shrugged. "Sixteen, I think." She peeked in the box with the empty light containers and then nodded. "Yes, sixteen."

"Did you put them all in one long cord, end to end?"

"No. I did half and half, so eight strung into one. Then I ran an extension cord up the trunk for the bubble lights and candles. I couldn't connect them together because they didn't have a receptacle end, only a prong end." LuAnn smiled smugly, proud of herself for knowing that much about electrical cords.

He made a face. "Well, it looks to me like you're pulling too much power from a single outlet. You'll either need to take the extension cord you used for the bubble lights and candles around a corner to another plug that happens to be on a different circuit, or remove a couple of strings of lights."

She was not going to remove any of the light strings. Not after the hours she'd spent winding them around branches and then hanging ornaments over the top of them. And she wouldn't take off the bubble lights or candles, either. "All right. I'll run an extension cord under the door to our office."

He made the same face. "Well..."

LuAnn rolled her eyes. "Don't tell me. That plug is on the same breaker as this one."

"Most likely."

Tears threatened. Such a silly reason to cry. But she wanted this Christmas to be perfect. The best ever. Blown breakers and cords strung from one end of the inn to the other did not fit her perception of *perfect*.

Brad folded his arms and studied the tree from top to bottom. "Tell you what, I'll check the breaker box. The electrician put a whole-house diagram next to the box. Every room and plug is marked with a specific breaker. The office might have its own separate breaker."

She sniffled. "All right. Thanks."

"Now..." His million-dollar smile briefly lit the space. "Come see what I have for you." He led her to the box and lifted it to the floor. "My aunts insisted you needed these things. Don't feel obligated to keep them, but since Aunt Thelma and Aunt Irene intend to pop in for soup on Saturday, I suggest having at least one out where they can see it."

LuAnn looked in the box and gasped with delight. "Oh, those dear ladies." His elderly aunts had become good friends to the new owners of Wayfarers Inn after a rocky start. But this gift was enough to erase any memory of ill will. She reached into the jumble of wadded old newspapers and withdrew one of six brass candelabra. The weight startled her, and she gripped it with both hands.

Even in the dim light flowing through the front windows on this cloudy day, the candelabrum shone with a fresh polishing. She turned a disbelieving look on Brad. "Are they sure they don't want to use these themselves?"

"They aren't even putting up a tree this year. They said it's too much fuss and bother." He glanced around the spacious café and lounge space. "But obviously the thought of decorating isn't a 'fuss and bother' to you. It looks like the North Pole exploded."

She chose to ignore his last comment. "If they're sure they won't want to display them, I'll gladly put them to use here. I can put one on the grand piano in the middle of the pine garland, another on the corner of the coffee bar, and—"

A tremendous crash sounded from overhead. Both Brad and LuAnn looked up to the long, railed landing, then looked at each other. She put the candelabrum on the bar and, without a word, dashed up the stairs. Brad thundered up behind her. They reached the second-floor landing and were met by the newly hired part-time housekeeper, Constance Stanfill.

The woman's hazel eyes were as round as a pair of full moons. "Did you hear that?"

LuAnn nodded, releasing a nervous laugh. "I imagine the neighbors heard it."

Brad pointed to Maple and Mum, the room at the end of the hall. "I think it came from over there."

LuAnn's heart raced as if she'd just finished a marathon. She'd run up and down the stairs so many times in the past few months, she knew the heavy *pound-pound-pound* wasn't from exertion. Real concern gripped her. With the Thanksgiving rush done and the Christmas rush yet to begin, only one guest resided under the inn's roof—Alice Busby, a self-proclaimed wannabe novelist who claimed she intended to stay in the Honeymoon Suite until she'd completed her very first whodunit. She was probably bent over a spiral notebook, scrawling red herrings with her pencil. If Constance hadn't created the noise, then who had?

Brad touched LuAnn's arm. "Stay here." He tiptoed to Maple and Mum and pressed his back against the wall next to the doorjamb. He pushed the door open slowly, his head cocked at an angle as if fearful something might leap out at him. Then his tense frame relaxed. He crossed the threshold. "Oh, boy…"

LuAnn darted to the room and looked in. The large, ornate mirror that had been hanging on the wall across from the bed lay shattered on the floor, its frame bent into a rhombus. She crouched and touched one shard of thick beveled glass. "Did the hanger come loose?" Their handyman, Tory

"Thorn" Thornton, was so careful about securing heavy paintings and mirrors to studs, but maybe the hanger hadn't been strong enough to hold the mirror. She remembered struggling to carry it to the car after buying it at Harry's antique store.

Brad scowled at the wall. "No. Thorn used two hangers instead of one, and both are secure on the wall."

"Then the wire we put on the back of the mirror must have come loose."

He picked up the misshapen frame. LuAnn could see that the eyebolts were still screwed into the thick wood, and the wire remained stretched across the back of the frame. Brad looked from the frame to the wall to the frame again. He frowned. "This didn't fall, LuAnn. It had to have been lifted from the hangers and dropped."

A Note from the Editors

We hope you enjoy Secrets of Wayfarers Inn, created by the Books and Inspirational Media Division of Guideposts, a nonprofit organization that touches millions of lives every day through products and services that inspire, encourage, help you grow in your faith, and celebrate God's love in every aspect of your daily life.

Thank you for making a difference with your purchase of this book, which helps fund our many outreach programs to military personnel, prisons, hospitals, nursing homes, and educational institutions. To learn more, visit Guideposts Foundation.org.

We also maintain many useful and uplifting online resources. Visit Guideposts.org to read true stories of hope and inspiration, access OurPrayer network, sign up for free newsletters, download free e-books, join our Facebook community, and follow our stimulating blogs.

To learn about other Guideposts publications, including the best-selling devotional *Daily Guideposts*, go to ShopGuideposts.org, call (800) 932-2145, or write to Guideposts, PO Box 5815, Harlan, Iowa 51593.

Sign up for the Guideposts Fiction Newsletter
and stay up-to-date on the books you love!

You'll get sneak peeks of new releases, recommendations from other Guideposts readers, and special offers just for you . . .
and it's FREE!

Just go to Guideposts.org/Newsletters today to sign up.

Guideposts® Visit Guideposts.org/Shop or call (800) 932-2145

Find more inspiring fiction in these best-loved Guideposts series!

Mysteries of Martha's Vineyard
Come to the shores of this quaint and historic island and dig in to a cozy mystery. When a recent widow inherits a lighthouse just off the coast of Massachusetts, she finds exciting adventures, new friends, and renewed hope.

Tearoom Mysteries
Mix one stately Victorian home, a charming lakeside town in Maine, and two adventurous cousins with a passion for tea and hospitality. Add a large scoop of intriguing mystery and sprinkle generously with faith, family, and friends, and you have the recipe for Tearoom Mysteries.

Sugarcreek Amish Mysteries
Be intrigued by the suspense and joyful "aha!" moments in these delightful stories. Each book in the series brings together two women of vastly different backgrounds and traditions, who realize there's much more to the "simple life" than meets the eye.

Mysteries of Silver Peak
Escape to the historic mining town of Silver Peak, Colorado, and discover how one woman's love of antiques helps her solve mysteries buried deep in the town's checkered past.

Patchwork Mysteries
Discover that life's little mysteries often have a common thread in a series where every novel contains an intriguing whodunit centered around a quilt located in a beautiful New England town.

To learn more about these books, visit Guideposts.org/Shop